Oliver Logan
and the Witness Tree

R. D. Slover

ISBN 978-1-64349-006-9 (paperback)
ISBN 978-1-64349-007-6 (digital)

Christian Faith Publishing, Inc.
832 Park Avenue
Meadville, PA 16335
www.christianfaithpublishing.com

Printed in the United States of America

This story is dedicated with much love to
my grandson, Oliver Logan Slover.

Contents

Part 1

Oliver Comes to Stay

I t was the best of times, and it was the worst of times. Whoa! That is entirely too corny, although some people might just have felt that way. That particular *and* peculiar phrase had come entirely to pass. But none of that was the case this day; on this day, it was simply one of those "times" that occur in people's lives. Sometimes, those times have a sort of splatter effect that affects not just one person, but rather several at once. *This* was one of those times if ever there was one.

Oliver Logan, less than three months away from his fourth birthday, was resting his forehead against the cool window of the vehicle while peering out the glass with his trademark big, wide open, little boy eyes. He was seeing just about everything, but barely noticing anything in particular. Oliver had been down this same road many times with his Pap going to visit Uncle Dave and Aunt Mary. So, despite his wide-eyed view of the journey, there was precious little, if anything new or interesting for him to see.

What made *this* day one of *those* times was the mixed bag of factors that had come together in the metaphorical "perfect storm" of events to find Oliver in his car seat in Uncle Dave's big grey truck. Sitting beside Oliver was Kathleen, the young lady of twenty-one years, previously his cousin who would become his big sister. In the front seats, Kathleen's parents, her Mom and Dad were Oliver's Uncle Dave and kindly Aunt Mary. There were others of course, but these four people were the ones most directly influenced by the afore-mentioned perfect storm of events that ultimately led to this day, the day Oliver went home to live with Uncle Dave, Aunt Mary, and Kathleen.

Oliver's new family lived in a big old house at No. 1 Hughes Street in the community of Rural Heights. That house was over a hundred years old and had a history almost as rich as the entire area that would now be Oliver's new neighborhood. Aunt Mary had been brought home to this house as a baby, and except for a few years away at college, she had lived there all her life.

To be sure, there was a host of people variously impacted by the range and scope of events that led up to this day, this moment, with a heavy dash of life tossed in for good measure. Without question, Oliver was the single most impacted person of all but his thoughts, as he rested his forehead on that window, can only be speculated on and sugges-tions made as to their nature. What do almost four-year-old boys day-dream about? Well, on this day, he was actually thinking on what he'd been told when Uncle Dave and his family drove up to collect Oliver and his belongings to take them all home. In a nutshell, Oliver was told that he'd be going to live with family that he knew but different from the family he'd lived with thus far in his young life. He was promised by Uncle Dave that although things were going to be different, they were still going to be good and maybe, just maybe even better.

Now, you're probably wondering why Oliver is going to live with family, but not his immediate family—his mom and dad. That's where this story initially takes a sad turn because you see, Oliver was on the verge of becoming an orphan before he was saved by Uncle Dave and Aunt Mary.

Tragically, Oliver's mom had just passed away unexpectedly at the young age of twenty-three years old, just two weeks before her twenty-fourth birthday. Oliver's biological father was one of those guys that shirked his responsibilities and was never around. In fact, before Oliver was even born, his dad had moved far away and was never heard from again.

Oliver's mom was a very pretty young woman named Melanie, and her dad was Oliver's grandpa, Pap. As luck would have it, Oliver and his mom were warmly welcomed into Pap's house, and they all lived together with Melanie's sister, Aunt Katie, and her two brothers, Uncles Andy and Brad. Aunt Katie was away at college a lot of the time but loved coming home to fawn and fuss over her new nephew.

Maybe Oliver's dad wasn't interested in being around, but his Pap, aunt, and uncles were all very happy to welcome baby Oliver home. A lot of the routine babysitting chores were shared by all of them and that included feeding Oliver his bottles, burping him, changing his diapers, and giving him baths too. Of course, there was more to taking care of baby Oliver, but these were the basic, most oft-repeated tasks, and everyone pitched in on all of them with one notable exception—Uncle Andy. He never changed a diaper, ever. He left that to Pap more often than not.

For the first two years of Oliver's life, everything was good at Pap's house. It was a small but busy place, and it seemed like there were always people coming and going. While his mom tended to Oliver during the day, Pap would come home from work and imme-diately assume responsibility of his cherished grandson. That often meant getting dressed for the weather and going out in Pap's old black truck.

A lot of times, they would take the long ride out to the coun-try where Uncle Dave and his family lived, and Pap and his brother would often just sit in the open air of the big garage where Uncle Dave kept the family vehicles. He had also set it up to be a rather impressive man-cave complete with big screen TV, refrigerator, and of course, a few comfy chairs. Sitting in the big open doorways of the garage, the two brothers could talk and keep an eye on the swiftly growing Oliver as he played and romped around the big yard.

Not only was the yard big, but it had several outstanding trees of various shapes and sizes. There were a couple of beautiful old oak trees and a maple with its distinctive leaf design. There was also a stand of nine really tall pine trees lining the driveway from the road up to the big garage, but of all the trees, their variety and sometimes colors, the best tree was right behind the back of the big garage.

Now, as it was related earlier, the garage was a big, impressive structure in itself. But standing back and looking at the garage from afar, one could not help but notice how big this spectacular tree really was. In a word, it was enormous, and it was often said if it were ever to fall and fall the wrong way, the garage would be a complete loss along with most of whatever was in it. Many was the time Uncle Dave was seen making the sign of the cross and pointing upward to heaven then back to that tree, especially after a bad storm or unusually strong winds.

Even without his real dad around, Oliver was a very happy boy. He was greatly loved by his family; every one of them was just tickled to be around him, and all were glad he was in their lives. But change was in the wind, and soon, events would occur that would shake Oliver's family to its very core. Needless to say, life was about to change for everyone you've heard mentioned thus far.

Oliver's Pap was getting ready to move to Canada and live there with his new wife. Oliver's mom was dating a nice, really smart fellow named Joe who was absolutely wonderful about holding Oliver, playing with him or taking care of him, and just being with the boy. Oliver had been seeing Pap a lot less because he and his mom were spending a lot of quality time with Joe and actually beginning the process of moving in together. It certainly looked like Joe was going to be Oliver's new dad, and everyone was glad about that.

Then, one day, came a terrible report, Pap had gotten home from work and gone to bed one hot summer night when there was a loud knock on his door. It was a local police officer who knew the family and all the kids in that house. It was his sad duty to tell Pap that his daughter, Melanie, had passed away earlier that day. This was terrible news, and she was so young! Oliver's mom was going to celebrate her twenty-fourth birthday in just two weeks, but a fatal heart flaw took her away. Pap was devastated, and his kids were stunned as well at the loss of their sibling. No one even knew what to say to Oliver who was just about to turn four years old in a few months.

Furthermore, what was to happen to Oliver now? Where would he live, and with whom? For various reasons, Oliver's present family, his immediate family, uncles, Andy and Brad, and Aunt Katie were not the answer, Joe was not the boy's legal guardian, and Pap—in preparation for moving to Canada—was selling the house everyone had been living in. Prayers were offered, a lot of prayers, and those prayers were received, reviewed and answered. Can we get a drum roll please and thank you . . . good old Uncle Dave and Aunt Mary stepped in and saved the day. Not only did they welcome Oliver into their home, but they changed their own lives by doing so.

By this time their daughter, Kathleen, had finished nursing school, she was starting a new job in that field and was twenty-one years old. With their only child now grown and starting her own life, it was also time for Uncle Dave and Aunt Mary to change their lives a little bit. Have more fun, go out more, and take those vacations that had been talked about, but never really happened. Despite looking forward to some carefree grown up time together, these two wonderfully generous people decided to make their house a home for soon-to-be four-year-old Oliver Logan. He was, as Uncle Dave proclaimed, family after all, being Uncle Dave's great nephew. Soon, these family dynamics would undergo a few changes and relationship status and titles, for some people would be altered forever and give everyone pause to think on their heretofore unspoken complexity.

But before we get into all that, there was the inevitable period of transition. Having a new person come to live with you is a lot different than having them come to visit. There were assignments to be issued. There were boundaries and rules that weren't in place where Oliver had lived before, most things were different. Those differences could be small or significant depending on what they were. Oliver now had a structured schedule where in the past there had been a much more flexible routine.

Bedtime was a struggle at first. Oliver wasn't much of a talker at this point in his young life, and his mother's as yet unsatisfactorily explained disappearance was bothering him. So was missing his Aunt Katie, Uncle Brad, Uncle Andy, and Pap not being around a lot more; he hardly ever saw them now. Kathleen was wearing several hats in her new role as first time sister, babysitter, and role model. Oliver had to learn about privacy from the ground up. Living at Pap's was a whirlwind at times, and with so many people in such a relatively small house, true privacy was a luxury seldom experienced there.

Life with his new family was good for Oliver. As he'd been promised, he simply needed a period of adjustment. He'd been through a lot for a young boy and had seen more serious changes than he could possibly be expected to handle. His frustration and sometimes not knowing how to handle these changes showed, and Oliver often acted out in various ways. But despite these difficult times, he was always surrounded by love, and he was loved from all his family near and far. Even so, there was a rather difficult period of transition, and everyone did their best to let Oliver come around naturally.

To that end, it was common for Oliver to play outside, and the great big yard held a lot of interesting things to see and do without getting in trouble. Aunt Mary could always keep an eye on Oliver as she worked around the house and in the kitchen. Frequently, she would also call out his name and wait for him to respond, just to keep him close by.

Oliver didn't have any real playmates because, not only was he new to the area, but the neighboring houses were sort of far away or so it appeared because every house seemed to have a fairly large yard around it. Thus, too far away for a four-year-old little boy to wander off on his own. But Pap was there sometimes, and Uncle Dave was always working out in the great big yard when he wasn't actually at his real job. One of Uncle Dave and Oliver's first favorite things to do together was to cut the grass with both of them mounted on that gallant steed that also served as a riding lawn mower.

Part 2

Oliver and the Trees

One day, Pap was visiting, and as he and Uncle Dave were sitting around talking, Oliver decided to climb into one of the trees in the yard. Uncle Dave had taken to kidding Oliver about his "big monkey feet," and as Oliver scampered up into the higher branches of the tree, his Uncle turned to Pap and nodded his head in Oliver's direction smiling and saying, "He is really at home now up in that tree. Too bad there aren't any bananas for him up there."

Both Uncle Dave and Pap shouted out to Oliver as he disappeared into the upper branches, "Please be careful and do not fall. Call us if you need help getting down."

Soon, Oliver was heard carefully making his way back down and into view. He stopped and sat on a sturdy branch leaning up against the trunk of the tree looking down at his Uncle Dave and Pap. Uncle Dave commented to him, "I told you that those were monkey feet. You should have seen yourself scamper up that tree like Cheetah from Tarzan."

This made Oliver smile; in fact, it made all three of them smile.

There were times when Oliver tried climbing in some of the other trees, and he developed a preference for certain trees that were easier to climb and get back down and out of. There were only a couple of trees deemed not so suitable for climbing. They were merely to be enjoyed for their beauty and shade, as trees should be regarded.

Obviously, it wasn't possible to climb the big old pine trees lining the driveway, but almost every other tree on this property was good for climbing.

Oliver spent the better part of his first summer's days out in the yard climbing in and out of the many different trees. For some reason, however, he never got around to climbing that giant eastern sycamore tree that stood proudly behind the garage. There was something about that tree that was a bit intimidating to Oliver. He looked at the tree every time he walked out of the house and even lay on the grass on his back looking up into its many, many branches. But he never actually climbed up into it.

Now, unbeknownst to Oliver, that old sycamore was watching him just as the boy was looking at the tree. The grand old tree had noticed Oliver the very first time he ever came to visit at No. 1 Hughes Street.

The old tree had seen everyone who had ever come to live or visit or even just to ask directions from the residents of the big old house. In fact, that venerable tree was so old, it actually predated the old house itself. No one knew exactly how old the giant tree was, and everyone who ever lived there simply knew that it had always been there too.

But that old tree did have a life, and a story that, if told, would encompass well over 150 years of local, national and world history. Oliver didn't know it, but there had been a few boys before him, and even a young girl or two, that would hear that story themselves, once the big old sycamore approved of them.

What? Well, truth be told, *all* of the trees in the yard were connected by a common location and a network that allowed them all to communicate through their root systems. Yes, the trees could always communicate with each other, and with people if they chose to, as young Oliver Logan was about to find out, much to his surprise and delight.

It was a nice, warm day in early July and just a few months before Oliver would celebrate his seventh birthday. Oliver came tearing out of the house headed for a cool shady tree to climb in which to eat the breakfast sandwich Kathleen had made for him. He started past the big old sycamore when he heard a strange rustling sound. He paused for a moment and looked around. There was no one there. He started to walk toward another tree, and he heard the noise again, seemingly louder, almost insistent that he acknowledge it. Oliver stopped, and as he was looking around, taking in everything in his immediate area, he felt something drop down on him. He looked, and the only thing he could see was a spiked ball with a stem on it. As Oliver stood transfixed gazing at the strange object, another one fell to the ground very close to the first one. Oliver looked up into the tree and absentmindedly took a big bite of his sandwich. Chewing steadily, the youngster was looking up into the tree, mapping a climbing route in his head as he mentally traversed up into the tree before actually doing so.

Oliver quickly finished his sandwich, and while still chewing his food, he began methodically climbing up into that great old tree. It was an easy climb, and the boy was silently asking himself why he'd never climbed it before. A strong voice, low in volume but perfectly discernible, spoke at that moment and said, "Because I've never invited you to climb in me."

Just like that! Oliver was stunned. The boy was very bright and had an active imagination developed over time as he played alone, but even he was taken aback by what he had definitely heard.

Oliver stopped climbing and asked out loud, "Did someone say something to me?"

There was no answer. The boy waited and strained to hear it again, but there was nothing—nothing but the breeze filtering through the many branches heavily laden with cool, shady leafage.

Oliver resumed his climb and soon reached a broad branch that was spread wide at the two pronged base where it came out of the tree and formed a natural seat. It was reasonably secure from falling, plenty of shade, and hard to see from the ground.

The boy nestled himself into that seat and began surveying his surroundings. It was cool and lush up in that tree hidden just a few feet off the ground. He felt secure, and he felt free of whatever was really bothering him; it was a good place. When he finally egressed that tree, he picked up the two sycamore balls and carried them into the house.

Many a time after that, Oliver took his meals up to that seat in the branches, and his love for that spot of complete peace and tranquility grew very strong. Oliver was growing and maturing in so many ways. His Uncle Dave and Aunt Mary were now Mom and Dad, and Kathleen was his sister. Oliver was very appreciative of Kathleen who had taken very good care of the boy when he first came to live with the family.

Through those often difficult days, Kathleen and Oliver became very close, and it was a very good thing for both of them. Kathleen used to reward her new "little brother" by inviting him into her room and watching movies or playing video games while eating snacks. As he grew up and began his own social circles and activities, and while his sister was at work or socializing, they didn't interact quite as much anymore, but they were still very close and as much friends as family.

Four more years quickly passed, and young Oliver was turning eleven years old, but he still sat up in the sycamore as often as he could, which was less and less. Oliver was active in sports almost year-round—soccer, swimming, and baseball too. He was also a pretty good student and liked hanging out with school friends as well. Despite growing up and having lots to do Oliver took a particularly nice day and made time to go sit in the tree. He had started occasionally taking books up with him to read, and he had brought one with him now. He was reading, *The Wind in the Willows*.

He got to his place and was soon nicely ensconced, marveling at the wonder of what that spot did for him, and it was then that he heard that voice again. "It's good to be with you again, Oliver."

He definitely heard it and should have been freaking out, but he was completely calm. Oliver did sit up a little, but still, he was surprisingly calm and composed when he replied with a query, "Did you say something to me once a few years ago?"

Oliver felt so connected to the tree at that moment that he imagined he felt the old sycamore smiling when it replied that it had indeed spoken to him, albeit ever so briefly. It was, the tree explained, a taste of things to come, possibly. The fact that Oliver was a very nice boy on the verge of growing into a fine young man was the deciding factor in all this. The older trees had watched with pride as he grew and developed, and they liked him. But Oliver was bound to the sycamore. That had been established long ago, and all the trees deferred to the seniority and greatness of the grand old sycamore.

So it was decided that the other trees should not talk to Oliver but rather the sycamore, and only the sycamore would be his teacher. That aged tree had done this before and was very good at teaching the lessons and passing on the knowledge. I suppose that was because of its age and location and because the tree had witnessed these events or felt them through its human pupils, those boys and girls, students from years gone by.

The great old eastern sycamore was connected to Oliver and had been connected to several of the previous kids who had found that wondrous seat in those lofty branches. These connections allowed thoughts to be shared when speaking would not suffice. In fact, connection sharing was the preferred method of communication. After all, no one can hear your thoughts, and there could be no risk of anyone hearing a tree speak, that wasn't supposed to.

Part 3

Ancient Arboreal Memories

And so the lessons began, and they began with the great trees first recollection, that of becoming a sapling. There was forest everywhere, and yet there was space for a new sycamore to put down roots. The young tree was directly influenced by those older trees surrounding him, and there were other younger trees as well. But the sycamore was a smart young tree and soon realized that it was best to pay attention to the older trees and listen to what they imparted to him. After all, they obviously know something, staying alive year after year, decade after decade.

The sycamore always paid attention and remembered seeing people for the first time. They were natives on a hunting party, and there were several of them. They had made camp near the sycamore but not close enough to be any sort of threat.

The Mingo hunters had gotten some game, a big deer, and were roasting it on a large hot fire that they kept burning by feeding it dead logs and broken up branches. This fire was the first the young and impressionable sycamore had seen, and the root system was humming with messages to all the trees reminding them that fire was their worst enemy.

The hunters were very appreciative of their received bounty and thanked the Great Spirit. It was explained by the older trees that these natives were rapidly being forced away from the lands they grew up on and lived on for many years. It was the year 1790, and these Mingo tribesmen were among the very last to be found in those parts since most of their tribe had moved to Ohio before the end of the eighteenth century. Settlers were spreading out and taking up land everywhere in the years around 1815, and to attest to the fact, there was a new road just down in the valley over the hill from the sycamore's roots.

Though it wasn't close enough to the edge of the bluff sycamore was situated on, or even simply tall enough to see, the other trees—who were in a position to see—reported what they were witnessing. There were wagonloads of people and possessions being pulled up that new road by cattle, horses, and even mules. People were walking behind the wagons too, all settlers heading west. Early travellers called this avenue the River Road because it led to and effectively ended at the banks of the Allegheny River.

Part 4

Panic Amongst the Trees

One day in the spring of 1815, all the trees heard another noise that was to become to them, a most unwelcome sound, axes felling trees and the grunts and groans of men working to clear out some land. Again, all this activity was down near the road over the hillside from where the sycamore was rooted. Those trees closest and with a view were horrified at what they saw. This was something completely new and a threat never before even imagined. These trees had lived in peace for many, many years, over a century for some of them. They had just gotten used to humans, but thought that they just passed by and never stayed very long, like the Indians that had been hunting years ago. They stayed but only briefly, and when they left, all they left was footprints. They honored nature and respected it, all the living things, plants and animals.

Now men were coming and killing the trees. The people didn't view it that way; they were simply building and improving their lives. But do not doubt for a moment that the trees viewed it differently, as nothing less than barbarism. The trees all knew that, occasionally, one of their numbers died. It could happen naturally by way of old age, or sometimes there were ravenous insects that simply devoured certain trees. It was understood and an accepted part of life in the forest. Ultimately, though, whenever a tree fell, its connection to the root system went silent, and its voice was never heard again. It was painful and difficult for the trees to lose friends in the name of human progress.

All the trees began wondering the same thing, and communications on the root line were humming. Would the humans soon be coming up onto the small bluff where they all stood and had stood together for decades? They received their answer soon enough.

The building down over the hill and right by the River Road was to be a post office and inn for weary travellers. The bluff the trees stood upon was an excellent viewpoint for some nefarious characters to watch and see who and what were about the inn. These were highwayman, robbers by any other name.

As Oliver was taking in all this information and formulating questions, he heard Aunt Mary calling him to come in for supper. He silently bid the tree goodbye and began the easy and very familiar climb down to the ground. As he walked toward the house, Oliver's young mind was racing, and he felt like tonight's table conversation would be unlike any of the seemingly countless previous meals with every family member present, there were interesting things to discuss.

And so it was, but Oliver, bright young lad that he was, didn't rush to the table all breathless and excited proclaiming that there was a talking tree was in their yard. No, instead, Oliver asked Aunt Mary questions regarding what she knew about the history of the area.

Since Aunt Mary had grown up in the house and spent most of her life living right there, she was indeed not only interested in the history of the area but also extremely knowledgeable about it too.

When Oliver mentioned Indians being in the area, everyone at the table was interested in what he had to say. The boy asked if there were Indians living on their property and what might have happened to them—where did they go? Aunt Mary was thrilled at this sudden turn of events. She had watched as Oliver grew from a sad, frustrated little boy into a very nice, intelligent schoolboy who asked great questions and easily carried on conversations with those older than he. This table chat about Indians and their neighborhood history was the beginning of a new and interesting chapter in all of their lives. Aunt Mary told Oliver and everyone else at that table all she knew about those Indians from long ago, and she even mentioned a couple of area tribes, including to Oliver's secret delight, the Mingo tribe.

That particular day was forever etched in Oliver's memory, but he was gently reminded that he had activities and responsibilities such as soccer practice and homework. For these reasons, the boy had to put off climbing back into the sycamore for several days.

Soon enough, the weekend came, and immediately after having a delicious Saturday breakfast at Dennis's—their favorite local diner—and then playing in his soccer game, Uncle Dave and Oliver returned home around noon. Kathleen was in the kitchen and made him a nice peanut butter and jelly sandwich, gave him a carton of chocolate milk, and Oliver was off to the old tree with his lunch in hand. Aunt Mary was in the living room cleaning, and she watched out the window with a silent, mysteriously contented smile as the boy who had come to steal her heart easily disappeared up into those lofty branches once again.

As he munched on his sandwich and drank his milk, the old tree casually welcomed Oliver back once again. The sycamore was not only old but wise as well and knew that Oliver had another life, a life that he was obligated to live and grow in, and it was fine that their visits had grown so few and far between. In his special seat, Oliver exuded a spirit of kindness and goodness that the trees in the yard had sensed from the time he first started playing in their midst.

Seamlessly, the sycamore resumed teaching the boy. The previous lesson had concluded just as the highwayman were hiding on the bluff watching for an opportunity to ply their illegal trade. The robbers were only the second group of humans to ever encamp up on the bluff, but the trees all innately sensed that these humans were different and up to no good, not that they could do anything about it.

The trees could only stand by as mute witnesses while the robbers schemed and put into operation their plans. After a couple of days of watchful deliberation, someone of interest arrived at the inn over the hill. That night, the five bandits silently crept down to the solitary building and snuck inside. No one is quite certain what happened once they entered the building, but everyone knew that their carefully laid plan had come completely unraveled once they were inside.

Gunshots were heard, and cries came out of the inn that night sometime after midnight. Soon, there were lanterns and torches being lit, and riders on horseback were coming and going in a hurry up and down the River Road.

The trees overlooking the scene below them related to those that could not see that only three of the five robbers walked out of the building, and they were tied up and pushed out by other men with torches and rifles. Soon, several riders arrived and took over all official conduct of the goings on there at the inn. These were soldiers from a military post several miles away, and they were the official law of the land at that time. They assumed custody of the tightly bound criminals who were forced to walk while the soldiers rode en route to wherever justice was going to be meted out.

There was undoubtedly more interest among the humans when this event happened, but the trees were affected too. They had just realized the difference between good people and bad. It would forevermore be interesting whenever people were in their midst as the venerable old trees and their companions on the bluff strove to recognize people for their goodness or otherwise.

The attempted robbery was, ultimately one of those unrecorded events in history, simply a side note to the overall history of this particular area.

However, things were about to change and do so quickly. More people were moving into the area, and along the road over the hill from the bluff, a great many trees were felled to make room and provide building materials for the new houses that were popping up all up and down the length of the road. The anguished cries of the trees being cut down was mingled with the shouts of the men as their ringing axes took down tree after tree. It was a terrible experience for all those trees that were left, and they never forgot as long as they lived, nor did they ever outgrow their fear that they might one day fall victim to the sharp axes people used.

With so many people now living in the area, it wasn't long before children found the bluff and began playing there. Soon after, the adults were introduced to the area and began picnicking up there in that cool, shaded grove of trees on the bluff. The grove was soon favored by people because of its beauty and shade. Almost every weekend during the warmer months of the year, there were people having picnics, people just coming to the grove to sit in the cool shade and read or even take naps.

Those were pleasant days to the trees that made up the grove, and this was in spite of the fact that more and more people were moving into the area and that meant more progress, more felled trees.

Many new homes were built, and there were also various businesses down along the old road over the ledge of the bluff. There were farms too, and that meant the clearing out of a lot of trees. Still, the grove on the bluff withstood all these developments. Then in the mid-1830s, coal was discovered in the area, the very immediate area.

Surveyors and mineralogists came in to examine this new discovery to determine whether this was a big find that could be exploited or not. The city of Pittsburgh was only fifteen miles away, and at this time, its people were consuming over four hundred tons a day. Coal mining in the greater Pittsburgh region was big business, and this local find was determined by experts to be a rich bituminous strike.

The road below the bluff was in constant use and was muddy and treacherous in the springtime, and cloudy with choking dust during the summer. There were few really good times to travel this important artery, but people had no alternative. Eventually, it became necessary to improve it to accommodate all the traffic it experienced every day of the year. As the road was widened, it became necessary to cut down more trees with the same sad effect on the survivors as always. Once that rough road was improved, it was also given a new name, one befitting its status as the main road to the first community in the area, it was called the Rural Ridge Road—named after that growing community down below the bluff, Rural Ridge.

Then, one day, several men came up onto the bluff and began surveying the land. None of the trees knew exactly what was going on, but there was a collective sense of despair amongst all of them. They would soon learn these important lessons though—no secrets last forever, "progress" is inevitable and not necessarily good for everything, and rarely do any of the really great spots go unmolested or unspoiled regardless of their beauty and supposed isolation. The natural, longstanding residents of the grove on the bluff were soon to find all of this out for themselves.

A curved, rather steep road was cut out of a hill that led from the main highway over the hill up to the bluff and beyond. The grove of trees was now between the cliff side and a new thoroughfare. Several more longtime members of that particular stand of timber were felled in the name of progress, and they were missed by their arboreal companions left yet standing.

The sycamore tree was, by now, over thirty years old and grow-ing strong and tall, a very good candidate for the work of the axe men. But happily, so far, the sycamore remained unscathed, steadily growing in size and scope.

Men were constantly coming and going every day, and soon, something happened that would change the grove forever. Across the valley, level with the grove; but on the opposite ridge, trees were cut down in great numbers, and a road was cut out of the forest there. But this was to be no ordinary road. By the care and amount of atten-tion this thoroughfare was getting from an army of workers, it had to be something more than just a road.

And it certainly was more than that; it was a railroad that when completed would impact the grove, its trees, and in fact, everything and everyone in the entire valley. Every tree recalled the first time it had experienced the intense, rumbling root shaking only a pass-ing train can give. For years, there it would be, two times a day. So reliable that you could set your clock or watch to it, as the train was always on time at noon and midnight, as it came to haul out coal by the carful.

Oliver was settled into his niche in that grand old tree feeling the information seep into him as the tree imparted its own historical lessons. The young lad took in all the information, and he was the center of attention at supper that night.

Oliver had an interesting way of initiating table talk during meals by asking his aunt and uncle specific questions designed to take a conversation down a particular path. His Aunt Mary was delighted because she also had a keen interest in the local history. After all, she had grown up in the house they now all lived in.

His Aunt Mary questioned Oliver as to where he had suddenly found this interest in the old coal mining days so long ago. It would have been difficult to tell her that he sat up in a tree and either heard or simply felt whatever that eldest member of their property's trees imparted to him. No, there was no need to be that honest.

Fortunately, the boy had actually heard bits and pieces of the coal stories from a couple of older neighbors as they sat out in lawn chairs, drinking something cool, and chatting it up about the old days in the neighborhood. His Aunt Mary was secretly thrilled at this new interest of Oliver's, and she shared what she knew that helped fill out the whole story initiated by that great old tree.

Aunt Mary went on to tell Oliver about the dark side of the area's coal mining history and the attempts to get better working conditions for example. Oliver thought that it would be in the mining company's best interest to look out for the welfare of its employees, those men who went deep down into the mines to bring out the valuable coal. But such was not the case, not at all.

School was over for the year, and Oliver was looking forward to three whole months of swimming, fishing with Uncle Dave, playing on a baseball team, and just being a kid out of school for the summer, living it up with his friends. And there would also be long lazy sessions just kicked back in his spot up in the sycamore. There would be more local history lessons as well, and Oliver liked the idea of such easy learning—and no tests!

Oliver was always a lean boy. He started out life with an ambitious appetite, and it was thought that he was going to be a bigger guy like his uncles and his mother's side of the family. However, one day, when he was around six, he simply lost that famously big appetite. There weren't any medical issues; the boy was just not a big eater after that age.

To that end, he grew up a wee bit on the slight side, but definitely a tall kid. Wiry and tall, Oliver was getting pretty good throwing a couple of different pitches that his Uncle Dave was showing him. Baseball season was upon them, and Oliver was going to try and be a pitcher. Tall, lean, and strong as well as being a southpaw. *This could be interesting to watch,* thought his uncle.

Oliver was an almost instant success during his first season playing organized baseball. Uncle Dave had prepared him well, not babying the boy with easy tosses back and forth. No, that sort of molly-coddling went by the boards as quickly as his uncle thought Oliver could handle that hard ball coming at him a little faster and harder each time they were out in the yard together. He pitched every third game and played first base the rest of the time. Overall, he might have been a better hitter, but it was only his first season.

Furthermore, another activity had caught Oliver's interest, and soon enough, like several of his friends from school, Oliver was an avid Cub Scout. He liked the books he had to read about the history and activities of Cub Scouting and looked forward to moving on to becoming a Boy Scout a few years down the line. Oliver was growing into a fine young boy, and his twelfth birthday would be celebrated in the coming fall. He was smart, polite, personable, and somewhat independent. By that, it is meant that Oliver did the right things without being told more often than not. He made his bed every day, kept his room reasonably clean, and did what was expected of him regarding chores. He was an active and busy kid, a happy one too. The trees had all seen the good that was in him, those innate qualities that can take time to nurture, time to develop, Oliver displayed those admirable traits much sooner than most kids.

The grand old sycamore was pleased whenever Oliver took the time to come and visit, but as we found out earlier, Oliver's many activities and responsibilities were taking up a lot of his time, and unbeknownst to Oliver, his time was running out.

It was late in July, a very hot July. In fact, that particular summer had set several daily heat records with temperatures in the nineties almost every day and several times into the hundreds and always with a lot of sticky humidity. This was another steamy hot day, and baseball season had ended that very afternoon.

Oliver's team had finished with a nine-win and nine-loss record. It was a young team with several first year players, and the two dads who coached were often heard talking in excited tones about the great potential this team had if all the kids came back to play the next summer. Oliver's play improved noticeably from the start to the end of the season, and those two pitches he'd learned from Uncle Dave served him well, he didn't lose a game he started pitching. Not bad for a first year player.

Jumping out of Uncle Dave's truck, Oliver didn't wait to go inside and take a shower. He put his baseball gear in the man cave, grabbed himself a frosty cold can of root beer, and climbed up into the cool hidden space of the sycamore. Uncle Dave watched the boy swiftly disappear into those lofty branches and thought to himself that temperatures in the tree might actually be cooler than air conditioning.

Listening for his uncle to go into the house, Oliver eased into his comfy spot and popped open the soda he'd brought with him. Taking a refreshingly long draught from the can, Oliver sat for a moment, savoring his soda. Once he'd swallowed his drink, Oliver softly spoke to the tree, asking several questions.

Silently, he received answers to his queries. No, the tree did not adversely feel cold or heat, with the notable exception being fire. The venerable sycamore could only communicate with Oliver if the boy was touching the tree or within the area covered by its branches and roots. The trees communicated with each other by way of the root line, and if they weren't physically quite close enough, vibrations worked quite well.

Trees have the ability to see for 360 degrees. That meant they saw everything that was happening around them, limited only by their location and height or lack thereof. And, yes, there had been others that sat in that very same spot and talked with and learned from the sycamore. Oh, and of course, the larger older trees had the best communication ability, naturally. In fact, communicative ability was considered such a special gift that only those trees that had lived for more than seventy-five years were capable of it. The sycamore remembered things as far back as those days when Indians hunted around there, but it couldn't communicate with anyone until just after the American Civil War.

Part 5

A Not So Civil War

The old sycamore started telling Oliver of a group of local men who began gathering in the grove to discuss the politics of the day. Soon, these men were bringing their large striped flag and hanging it from a branch on one of the other larger trees. These men spoke passionately about their cause, and one could easily tell by observing the younger men in attendance, that such enthusiasm was infectious.

Within a few weeks, these gatherings took on a more somber, serious tone, even more so than before. War had been declared, several southern states had seceded from the union, and the president, Abraham Lincoln, had called for seventy-five thousand volunteer troops to bring those states back into the national fold. Several of the men and boys that were meeting under the branches of the grove had already enlisted and would be going away for army training very soon thereafter.

One warm spring night, while another gathering of the local men and older boys was going on, a younger lad of seven years had snuck up into the now very lofty, very mature sycamore tree. The spot that Oliver now comfortably melded with wasn't there in those days, it would develop later, but the tree did have some wonderful branches especially for hiding and eavesdropping. This resourceful boy, James Andrew, Jimmy as he was universally known, soon found his own spot after exploring that sturdy tree.

There were weekly meetings and enlistments as young men came of age and others terminated their personal civilian affairs to take up arms in the cause of their country, and Jimmy never missed one. There was an indescribable feeling that only those nights with the great flag of the republic, the soldiers in uniform, and the excitement as fellows congratulated each other and awaited their muster orders could bring. Those men, gathered for such a martial purpose, would seem as giants by their shadows cast from the large bonfires.

One week before that much anticipated muster date, Jimmy's older brother, Davey, turned eighteen. When Davey awoke that birthday morning, he went straight to the nearby military camp and enlisted. That day, Jimmy couldn't have been prouder of anyone than he was of his brother. The following week fairly flew by, and, on a bright, sunny Monday morning, those new enlistees gathered at the train station to be sent off in grand style with an adoring crowd, bands playing, and more. Flowers were strewn on the railroad tracks, ladies and girls were crying and waving, and fathers and the older fellows were speaking patriotic words of encouragement to these soldiers-to-be through the open windows of the slowly departing train. And just like that, the fellows were gone. Oliver knew from history class at school that the time being described was the spring of 1861.

After his brother left for the army, Jimmy didn't come down to the grove much. The early days of the war had seen a lot of excitement but that enthusiasm was misplaced. This "War Between the States," as it was also known, was not going to be over quickly. In fact, it might go on for years if indeed the Union won the war at all.

The first big battles were seemingly all won by the Confederate armies, and the Union or northern armies had looked very bad in defeat. Casualties, those wounded or killed in the war, began to come home in numbers that created shock and outrage amongst an unprepared public. Those healthy young men and strapping young boys that marched heroically off to war were coming home in coffins or, if they were alive, many were missing limbs or were terribly scarred for life in other ways. There were precious few Union victories, and although they had seen the Confederates leave them in possession of the field at Antietam and claimed victory, it was really a tactical draw. It had become and remains the bloodiest single day of combat in American history. Fighting raged from dawn until dusk, and when it was mercifully over, this one day of violent conflict had caused over twenty-three thousand casualties. But the worst was yet to come, even in victory.

Very early in the especially hot month of July 1863, news came to the area of a fierce battle being fought right there in central Pennsylvania, in and around the small farming community of Gettysburg. Confederate General Robert E. Lee had once again led his Army of Northern Virginia northward across the Mason-Dixon Line in a bid to win a major victory on northern soil. It was hoped by the Confederate government that such a victory would entice either or both Britain and France to officially recognize the South's independence and openly offer them much needed military aid.

The Rebels were denied that victory after a bloody three-day battle that remains the biggest military event ever seen on the North American continent. In the end, on the night of the fourth of July, in a driving rainstorm-for-the-ages, those defeated Southerners began their tortuous retreat back into Virginia. Many Northerners, including President Lincoln, wanted victorious Union General George Meade to try and end the war right then and there, but his army was as battered as their defeated foe, and consequently, Meade began his pursuit of the retreating Rebels too late to be effective.

Losses on both sides were incredible, and altogether, there were over 150,000 men in the combined armies fighting on those fields all around Gettysburg. Of that total, the combined casualties of killed, wounded, or missing were well over 50,000 men, a full third of the total troops engaged. Back home, every day, local men and boys were delivered horribly wounded or in a pine coffin. There was hardly room for cargo other than these pitiful casualties of that horrible conflict.

Jimmy saw these things as he perched in that sycamore high enough now that he could easily see down into the valley below the bluff and across the valley to the opposite ridge where the railroad station and platform were. The sycamore sensed something was amiss with the boy. He never really relaxed and was never content to simply be sitting in the coolness of the tree. Rather, Jimmy was somehow agitated, fidgety, and he grew more so every day. The sturdy, mature sycamore instinctively tried to communicate something soothing to the young lad, but it didn't happen. Oh, how the tree was so close to being ready to communicate, but not just yet.

After several days of this fruitless waiting had gone by, one afternoon, the train arrived with more *special cars,* and Jimmy scampered down from the tree and ran to meet the train as it slowed to a stop. This day, the boy's parents were on the platform, and there were several other local families waiting with them. Each of those families was awaiting the arrival of a dead soldier. A father, husband, brother, son, maybe an uncle. Sometimes, one soldier was all of these things at once. Jimmy watched in silent shock and sadness as his brother, Davey, killed at Gettysburg the second day, arrived in his casket and was carefully down loaded off that long train of sorrow. Jimmy and his family took his brother away for the funeral, and, afterward, he returned to the grove, and the boy climbed back into the sycamore one more time. Not a word was said although much was felt and the boy never returned to the tree again.

In fact, however, there was one more, happy day when the trees in the grove were almost all full of gawking youngsters hoping for a better view. Down in the valley, along the old road, came a huge parade. The long difficult days of Civil War were over. After four terrible years, the North had eventually won, and the victorious troops had finally come home. Eager and excited young eyes peered out of the trees as the band led the way. Playing loudly and proudly, the drums and flutes beat out patriotic songs and victory songs too. The band was followed by row after row of local fellows who had "seen the elephant" in the service of their country. These men, now veteran soldiers, in their bright blue woolen uniforms followed a large, unfurled national banner and their regimental colors. They carried rifled muskets with burnished barrels and fixed bayonets gleaming in the bright sun as they proudly marched past the enthusiastic crowd that was getting hoarse from constantly cheering.

Oliver had both quite a bit to think about *and* talk about at supper and when his feet touched the ground. As he turned away and stepped toward the house, he casually patted the trunk of that remarkable sycamore.

Part 6

Coal Mining in the Area

Both Aunt Mary and Uncle Dave affirmed his stories about the area during the Civil War. It was well known in the community those families that had served America during her wartime crises. If you hadn't heard it through casual conversation, all one had to do was visit the local cemetery, which was abundant with marked war graves, mostly centered round a tall, imposing old statue of a Union soldier standing eternally vigilant over his fallen, or sleeping "pards." They also told him that the pre-war coal business, at that time, was about to ramp up production again in response to the exceptionally great demand for coal needed by the burgeoning steel industry. This was news that would soon have a direct impact on the grove up on the bluff and its current stand of trees.

Sometimes, Oliver would be lying on his bed or just sitting around, and he'd have random thoughts of questions he wanted to ask the sycamore when he climbed up that tree next time. He was trying to recall all of those thoughts of questions the next day as he climbed into his arboreal loft once again. Getting comfy, Oliver was immediately grasped by the feeling that *if* this tree were capable of laughing, it just had, at the very least, it seemed to chuckle. This feeling was followed immediately by a repeated message that the tree did not feel the cold of winter or the heart of summer nearly as much as people did. Things like losing its bark or leaves in the fall was painless too, it was just a natural cycle of the tree's life. No tree was immune to physical pain though; things like the woodsmen's axes or fire were too terrible to even contemplate. Oliver felt somewhat remiss because the tree had previously informed him of its immunity to the change in seasons and temperatures.

Willowy. That was the image the sycamore was using to describe Oliver and his movements, as observed by all of the trees in the yard. The boy was growing, but he had yet to experience those awkward growing pains that often made kids ungainly, a physical condition sufferers were eager to put behind them. Oliver slid into his spot up in those branches as naturally as one could imagine humanly possible. The tree felt his comfortable proximity, and both parties were silently pleased. There was that very pleasant, mutually shared and sublime experience between the boy and this tree.

As Oliver lay back in absolute comfort munching on the Twizzlers he'd brought along, that old sycamore once again began its muted narration. The coalmines were doing a booming business, and their related facilities were being built or expanded. This included many small homes that the company rented to its workers. These were in various little communities all over the area with the miners living in the hamlet closest to the mine they worked in. There was a company store that supplied all of the working families their most basic needs, but *everything* was owned by the coal company. The workers *and* their families were looked upon merely as labor, low wage slaves and little if anything else essentially. The lives of the workers and their families were of little consequence to the mining companies who hired brutal men to supervise, dominate, and intimidate every aspect of these people's abjectly miserable lives. These were less than honorable men, no more than paid thugs, whose control of every aspect of these people's lives led to widespread abuses and cruelty.

In many instances, the workers were so hopelessly indebted to their bosses and the mining company that, in reality, they were working for free. They had fallen behind in their rent and owed at the company store as well, and there was no end in sight to their plight, nothing to look forward to. Any attempts to break out of this seemingly endless circle of misery was harshly cracked down upon. Those brutal guards and enforcers would beat the workers mercilessly. They would go to the workers houses and dispose of and abuse the families. Even speaking about such things as unions was a dangerous thing. Once the workers were fired, they were forced off mining company property and often blackballed from working anywhere else in the area.

Nevertheless, those horrible conditions were frequently challenged, and actually, a couple of unions were in place. But they were in competition with each other rather than working toward a common good for their members. It wasn't until 1890 that these disjointed satellites merged to form one strong union. That was and still is the United Mine Workers Union. There were still the shanty towns where the miner's lived with their families but their lives, the overall quality of their lives was greatly improved. There was still significant physical danger in coal mining, but at least the new benefits made it more worthwhile than it had ever been for their predecessors.

Part 7

The Grove Is Changed Forever

One day, when the leaves were past turning colors and had now begun falling off their trees in earnest, a couple of fellows arrived at the grove. After looking about and discussing a few things, these men began walking around closely examining the trees that made up the grove and marking certain ones with a large red X. A few days later, several more people rode up to the grove in horse drawn carriages. When they stepped out and began casually walking through the trees, one woman seemed to be leading everyone else; at least the rest followed her everywhere she went. The trees in the grove were all in agreement that there was something different about this particular human.

A few weeks passed and despite a great snowfall just a few days earlier, several men, from the community that had grown up down in the valley just over the bluff where the grove stood, came up to the grove one frosty morning in late January 1898 to organize some sort of rally. Those taller trees as well as those who were situated close enough to the edge could see that it was going to be another military celebration and would be going on down in the village as well as up in the grove. There were placards tacked up on every pole around, displayed in every first floor window and the trees weren't immune to having these posters tacked onto them as well.

The local band was once again loudly playing patriotic and martial tunes, and soon, the young men who had enlisted came

45

marching down the road, around the hairpin curve and up the yet-to-be-named road to the grove. There a huge bonfire blazing just off that road away from the trees, and tables of food and warm beverages were now situated throughout the grove for all to enjoy. Speeches were made, dire threats of physical harm to be meted out with extreme prejudice were directed toward the Spanish, and several popular old war songs were belted out by the assembled multitude with great gusto. Certainly, none of the trees could read, but if they could, they would have known that nearly every one of those posters cried out, "REMEMBER THE MAINE!" The United States was about to be involved in what would be known as the Spanish–American War.

Later in the spring of that same year, men came to the grove with axes, saws, and wagons. Crews of these men literally attacked the pristine stand of trees, and it was soon evident that the hereto-fore mysterious red "X" was essentially the mark of death. As those doomed trees were felled, they were further set upon by men with smaller axes who trimmed them down. Branches were hacked off and quickly evaluated for useful production or to otherwise be turned into bundles of firewood. Quickly, the trees were reduced to long branchless poles to be hauled away and further fabricated at the local lumberyard. As soon as all that wood was removed, another crew came in to pull up the stumps of those once great trees. When there was a sufficient number of these stumps pulled from the ground, they were piled high and set ablaze. That fire was kept going by fresh stumps being tossed atop them on a regular basis. In a matter of days, at least two of every three trees living in the grove had been taken down. For several days, those surviving trees seemingly stood mutely by, but the root chain was alive with frantic speculation. Indeed, what exactly was coming next?

Several days later two horse drawn carriages once again labored up that steep hill to the now ravaged and wide-open former grove of trees. Once again, that particular lady stepped out and assumed command. She pored over some papers that a man produced and laid open for her perusal. She would look at the papers, look over the landscape and point with her forefinger for various reasons. The visitors spent considerable time talking and walking over the newly cleared grove. The woman walked over and stood on the edge of the bluff with these men and pointed to several things, but none of this made much difference to the trees that were there that day for they had no way of understanding it all. They would simply have to wait and see what was going to happen next. The sycamore had no way of knowing it, but undisturbed growth over the past hundred years had made this gentle giant one very beautiful tree. Ample room to grow and develop well-shaped branches and a strong root system had enabled the sycamore to age gracefully and become *the* tree everyone who visited the grove marveled at, and there were still several other very fine trees too.

When the weather turned fine in mid-spring, men armed with tools and workhorses returned to the grove with a purpose. There were two types of human that the trees could discern, those who constantly looked at big papers and told other men what to do, and there were the men who actually did the work. Initially a large, rectangular area, ten feet deep was dug out and the earth hauled away in wagons.

Large cut stones had been carted up to this work site, and the men labored to place those great carved stones around the perimeter of this foundation that would soon become a basement. Next, floorboards were laid in place and then a skeleton framework atop that. Then another ceiling and upstairs floor were completed while highly skilled craftsmen worked their magic finishing the first floor of what was to become a rather grand house. As the second floor ceiling was created, there would be atop that an enormous unfinished attic with a high-pitched ceiling and rough, unfinished wood.

The inside of the house was finished quickly, but the work was not hurried. Indeed, the woman the trees had felt was somehow different was the wife of the mining company president. She was a combination of influential power, privilege, and great kindness. It was under her direction and as a result of her insistence on quality craftsmanship that this great house, once just drawings on paper had come to be real, to exist here in the grove, to share space with the trees that had been deemed worth keeping on the property. Yes, property. The grove had been bought and paid for and was now to be the home and exclusive domain of one family. Within four months, the house was completed inside and out, and after the enormous roof was shingled, a great celebration was scheduled to acknowledge the builders' achievements, the completion of No. 1 Hughes Street. It was the number one address because it was the first house built up there, and it was called Hughes Street after Mr. and Mrs. Hughes, the first family who owned the mining company and were the builders of the house.

Once again, the grove was alive with raucous activity and huge bonfires at night. Musical bands were playing all day one after the other and into the night, and the amount and variety of food and drink was indescribable. All of the neighbors for several miles surrounding the house were invited along with the workers and their families. Everyone had a tremendously good time, and the occasion was the topic of conversation for years afterward.

Within days after the celebration, the owner of the mining company and his wife moved into the huge house that was not yet quite a home. The new residents spent their time collecting enough furniture to fill up the many large rooms in the house. The lady of the house had a lush grass yard created along with several beautiful little gardens of shrubs, roses, and other attractive plants. Everything planted was researched to succeed and thrive in the overall shade of the remaining trees in the newly developed grove up on the bluff.

These generous new owners were a different breed from previous mine owners, and their workers soon had cause to celebrate their current boss. Though unable to have children themselves, the couple loved kids and celebrated the birth of their employees' offspring by having a yearly celebration for all those born the previous year. Every kid got a birthday party, and although it wasn't necessarily on their actual birthday, it was a big party that was lots of fun and every child received a nice gift. During these celebrations, it wasn't unusual at all for some random youngster to work his way up into the branches of that old sycamore, it was such a natural thing to do.

Part 8

Doctor Wilson, I Presume

Despite the joy that the mining owner and his wife felt for and brought to their worker's children, as was revealed earlier, they could not have a child of their own. This eventually became a problem for the couple and they went their separate ways. The mining company was sold again, and the new owners, in 1910, turned the grand house over to the company doctor, old Doc Hugh B. Wilson who would live on the second floor while the first floor became a sort of hospital. This senior gentleman was unmarried but very busy and energetic, and he would need all of both qualities.

Despite increased safety measures overall, mining was still a very dangerous occupation and accidents frequently occurred both down in the mines as well as outside in the company yard near the railroad. Combined with this was the fact that other injurious mishaps occurred randomly and almost naturally, *and* the good doctor and his lone nurse assistant were expected to deliver babies along with everything else. So, for the next few years, the trees atop the bluff saw a near endless parade of patients and other people going in and out of the doctor's office. Countless times, fathers with expectant mothers went in and later came out with little bundles. Broken arms and legs, casts and splints, even rashes and burns—the doctor and his nurse treated them all. Often, entire families were at the hospital and the siblings or children would stay outside and play in the yard. It should come as no surprise that several little boys made their way high up into the sycamore's abundant branches hiding, just climbing or simply trying to escape the steamy summer heat.

Life in Rural Ridge took on a pleasant yet rather mundane quality. The days of summer passed by languidly and the bitter cold and snowy days were passed beside warm fires with nice, hot drinks. There was sled riding down fast tracked paths made so by local kids continually using them. There was an old Indian game played out on the thickly frozen ice of the local pond. There were sleigh rides in the snow up the hill and past the beautiful property at No. 1 Hughes Street. The years passed by serenely, and life seemed like it would always be peaceful and slow paced.

But this was a smaller rural community outside of Pittsburgh, and as idyllic as it seemed there, the world was a vastly different place. Beginning in August of 1914, the Great War, or World War I—as we know it today—was raging in places like Europe, Africa, the Middle East, islands in the Pacific Ocean, China, the Indian Ocean, and off the coastlines of North and South America, it truly was a worldwide war.

Part 9

The Great War

President Woodrow Wilson had won the 1916 Presidential election by campaigning to keep the United States out of this worldwide conflagration. However, it was now the spring of 1917, and repeated offenses by Germany—in particular—and their frightening new weapon, the submarine or U-boat as they were called, made America's neutrality a thing of the past. In April of that year, the United States entered the war, and nothing would ever be the same again, anywhere.

The old fellows, who had fought in the Civil War, fell in beside their younger veteran compatriots from the Spanish-American War. There were even a couple of fellows who had in their youth, ventured out West and fought in the Indian Wars for the United States Cavalry, and they all gathered at the local VFW (Veterans of Foreign Wars) resplendent in their old uniforms. Oh, but it was a loud celebration in anticipation of the coming parade and festivities later that day. Beers were hoisted on high, and many toasts were made both to the veterans that had been to war and these new, young warriors who were going overseas and into harm's way in the nation's service. The veterans were gathered in their uniforms to honor, inspire, and send off their sons, their brothers, cousins, and neighbors. Those aging veterans knew something of what these young men were going off to face, and they were proud of them, and also greatly concerned though they kept such trepidations to themselves. What every man in that VFW was really cheering for was the day, sooner than later, these new warriors would get to come home safely. They also hoped that this latest, soon to be greatest conflict in world history, would be the last of its kind to plague humanity.

Early that afternoon everyone for miles around had come out to see that the troops were sent off in style. In the distance, down the road around the bend once again, there came the strains of music, growing ever louder as they moved closer. The bands leading the marching troops played a selection of military, patriotic, and martial tunes that stirred every American patriot's heart. The troops that followed in their light brown uniforms and peculiar "doughboy" helmets were going by train to Georgia where none other than General John "Black Jack" Pershing personally named them his "Iron Division." Following training in Georgia and sailing overseas, these men went on to distinguish themselves in several key battles of the war.

Being from Pennsylvania, the Keystone State, they adopted a red keystone as their divisional patch, and that distinctive red patch, particularly the men who wore it, was soon spreading fear among their German foe on the battlefields of France.

Once again, in the warming weather of late spring, the trees were alive with bursting buds and young boys clamoring for a better view. At the end of town, there was a huge picnic set up for the new troops and their cheering supporters. Speeches were made, old oaths of doing vile things to this barbaric new enemy, the Germans, were uttered anew, and everything concluded with the singing of "America the Beautiful" and "the Star Spangled Banner." As the fellows boarded the trains, the throng continued singing such emotionally gut wrenching songs as "Amazing Grace," and one would have been hard pressed to find anyone who had dry eyes. The singing and cheering went on in earnest until the trains had departed and gone out of sight.

The old doctor stood on his porch and watched in silent despair as those brave and ebullient young men almost cheerfully went off to war and an uncertain future. He had been a surgeon in both previous wars and knew all too well the horrors these brave young fellows were about to encounter, at least he thought he did. Most of the veterans also thought they had seen the worst of it, of war's horror. Doc Wilson stepped off of his porch and walked to the edge of the bluff overlooking the valley and community below. He lit his pipe, and, leaning on a sturdy old oak tree, he puffed away and mused about every young man he personally knew that had left on that train. Why, he himself had delivered quite a few of them as babies some years ago, and he thought back on his own youth, what he was like at eighteen years of age. He tapped out his pipe bowl and sadly walked back to the porch and into his hospital. He hoped no one needed medical attention on that day as he was too depressed and simply wanted to be alone for the rest of the day. Some other, older members of that arboreal community silently pondered how many of those young soldiers had once been the young boys climbing up in their branches exactly like the youngsters had done this day. Indeed, they wondered about all the boys who had, at one time or another, made their way up into those lofty branches for a better look.

Part 10

Oliver's Busy Life

L ate that afternoon, as Oliver exited his nook up in the old sycamore upon hearing Aunt Mary calling him to supper, he was all but overwhelmed by today's lessons; history was one of the boy's least favorite subjects in school, but after several sessions up in the tree learning firsthand about the history of this immediate area and how it fit into overall American history, he was beginning to warm to the subject after all. Furthermore, this was exciting stuff to discuss over supper, and it was working to develop an even closer bond between Oliver and his Aunt Mary.

For the old trees part, there was a sense of urgency beginning to creep into this equation. Oliver had become very busy with sports, school, Cub Scouts, and other social activities. There was an unspoken rule that the tree was keenly aware of, but none of the people affected were ever cognizant of it. The rule was simply that all communication or related interaction between a tree and a human had to end before the child became a teenager.

Oliver's birthday was October 1, and that was just two months away. Two months until this remarkable young boy was twelve years old. While it wasn't absolutely necessary that the tree impart all of these lessons to Oliver, in some inexplicable way, it wanted to. The old sycamore, in its own arboreal way, yenned to complete this unusual task before time ran out.

Soon enough, summer was over, Labor Day was a very recent memory, and Oliver went back to school, and all the activities that occurred every school year. Despite a busy schedule that saw his time occupied almost all day and seemingly every day, Oliver, or perhaps it should be noted that his aunt and uncle, had decided he would start music lessons. This busy young fellow was about to become even more so.

While Oliver eagerly embraced piano lessons despite being pretty busy already, those who had ears were not so enthusiastic about the cacophony of sounds he was producing, all in the name of practice. As his uncle cruised around on his riding mower cutting the grass one last time toward the end of September, he was silently smiling, both inside and outwardly. He couldn't hear anything coming from within the house as he blissfully rode around on that noisy riding mower, with his protective headphones on. Aunt Mary and Kathleen, busy working in the kitchen, watched him outside, and both were silently quite envious of his obvious solitude and relative quiet.

On his birthday, Oliver went out to the tree and assumed his spot. Once there, he reached down out of the still leafy branches below where Kathleen was waiting and reaching up to hand him a paper plate with a big piece of his birthday cake and a pint of chocolate milk. He realized he couldn't stay long since there were guests and obligations the boy was accountable for. In that light, the old tree simply reveled in the boy's company and nothing but peaceful quiet was shared between them that day.

Soon, all the trees began dropping their leaves, and once again, it was time for Oliver and Uncle Dave to rake them into big piles and then bag them up. It was an exceptionally large yard, and there were several trees constantly dropping their leaves—it was a process that could take a few weeks, but the work had to be done nonetheless. Uncle Dave was nothing short of meticulous about maintaining their house and home, but he was particularly fastidious about keeping his huge property looking good.

All that autumnal yard work was silently witnessed by every tree on the property, and it was only the trees themselves who were aware that those halcyon days of summer and "communicating" with a human ended with the first frost. Oliver had never climbed into any of the trees after they lost their leaves. There was no particular reason for this on his part, that's just the way it was, but it was probably a good thing. The only obvious explanation for this was simple enough—warmer weather held the key for every tree. Warmer weather brought forth new life everywhere and to the trees, their innumerable new buds elicited hope and continuance for all the living things around them. Spring was the renewal season, and, gradually, that old sycamore tree emerged from its silent hibernation and boldly displayed an ever growing umbrella of brand new leaves, buds bursting open, and those tender new leaves unfurling into beautiful green leaves that would provide cool shade for everyone who sat under a spacious tree or up in it.

By the time the school year ended, Oliver was more than halfway to his twelfth birthday. But first, there was another glorious summer of baseball, Boy Scout camp, swimming, fishing with Uncle Dave, and no piano lessons to be experienced. The old sycamore patiently waited every day while Oliver was busily doing all the activities on his hectic schedule.

Busy though he was, Oliver never forgot about that old tree. He warmly patted its rough bark each time he walked past, it and in the recesses of his mind, the boy longed for some free time to literally just go hang out in those lofty branches. That opportunity came on a day that was so hot all activities were cancelled. Despite the intense heat, one couldn't even go swimming because there had been reports of heat lightning in the area.

Oliver's friends had all gone home to retreat into their houses, those bastions of cold, air-conditioned comfort. Although he had been invited and could go to any of his friend's houses practically any time, he opted to stay home and visit an old friend that lived nearby. After taking a long, cooler than usual shower, Oliver made two peanut butter and jelly sandwiches, grabbed a small bag of Doritos and a pint carton of chocolate milk, and headed out to the tree. With all of his food items in a brown paper lunch bag secured in his teeth, Oliver had both hands free to climb into his spot in the very noticeable cool shade. The old sycamore almost breathed as the boy slid into place and began eating his lunch. It was an experience no one could possibly understand or would even believe for that matter but the two of them, the old tree and the young boy, spiritually melded whenever they were together, and it was genuinely good for both of them. When Oliver had finished eating and bagged up his trash, the sycamore began once again.

The United States was in the war for just a little over a year and a half and on November 11, 1918, at 11 a.m. on the dot, the armistice was signed and the most destructive war, resulting in the greatest loss of life in recorded human history, officially ended. Bells were ringing, and people were dancing in the street and shouting joyously. There were great parades in the bigger towns, and cities like Pittsburgh and the little town below the bluff, celebrated as well, albeit on a much smaller scale. The fellows down at the VFW were celebrating and planning a big event when the local boys came home. But that wouldn't happen for a few months when the weather would be better for such an event.

One day, not long after Armistice Day, the train from Pittsburgh pulled in, and several fellows were helped off onto the platform. These young veterans were all in wheel chairs with no two having the same affliction. One was missing a leg, one was blind, another had no arms, and it went on like this for several weeks as the wounded men slowly trickled home.

The older veterans thought they'd seen the worse of combat, especially the now elderly Civil War vets. What could be worse than standing shoulder to shoulder on a broad front, firing muskets at another group of men massed together in a similar formation? But the gods of war had upped their game and the technology used in World War I was lethal on an unprecedented scale. Furthermore, diseases had once again run amok in the training camps and in the trenches, killing more soldiers than the actual combat did. There were a few caskets that had also come home on the trains but not nearly as many. The reason being that most American soldiers killed in World War I were buried by the grateful French, in France, where they had fought and died.

Several of the fellows who had come back maimed went up to see old Doc Wilson, and he immediately got involved in their special needs. If someone needed a specific prosthetic, Doc procured it for them. If a fellow suffering from mustard gas poisoning needed treatment, Doc did the best he could. Some of the medical issues the wounded troops suffered were heretofore totally unknown to the good doctor, such as the mustard gas, but Doc read and learned all he could so that he was at his best treating these wounded warriors, all of whom he regarded as his boys.

Regrettably, these new medical challenges and Doc Wilson's age proved to be obstacles too difficult to overcome, and in the midsummer of 1919, he suffered a fatal heart attack. There were newer medical facilities in the area, and the powers in the mining company hierarchy decided not to replace him, effectively eliminating his position in the company. The once grand house at No. 1 Hughes Street was now empty and in danger of falling into disrepair. The once finely manicured lawn had long since lapsed into just a yard that desperately needed weeding and regular mowing. The once pristine gardens were a complete loss and the many leaves that fell from all the trees on the property went uncollected that year. Thankfully, a new family, with several children, was looking to move into the area, and that empty house happened to suit their needs perfectly. One year after Doc Wilson passed away, the once ever-active edifice was about to come alive again, this time with the joyous raucous sounds only a large, happy family can create.

Part 11

The MacKelveys of No. 1 Hughes Street

The MacKelvey were an immigrant Irish family whose patriarch was an excellent carpenter. They were Mr. and Mrs. MacKelvey along with their seven children, five boys and two girls ranging in ages from seventeen to five years old. Mr. MacKelvey was universally known as Mac, and his arrival in America and purchase of No. 1 Hughes Street on June 1, 1920, was both timely and fortuitous. Not only was Mac a superb carpenter, but his four eldest sons were all quickly becoming noteworthy woodworking artisans as well. In short order after moving in, those industrious fellows had repaired everything that needed fixing in the house including putting up walls in the huge attic that created four more rooms!

Meanwhile Mrs. MacKelvey, known as Mama Mac, took the lead outside, and with every spare child helping, soon had the yard mowed, weeded, and raked up. Mama Mac regrettably conceded that it was too late that summer for any kind of garden, but she scanned the property with a trained eye and knew exactly where various components of her garden plans would be located next year. In silent observation, those long standing trees that had always lived up on the bluff were grateful for the newcomers and the stability this hard working family brought with them.

Mac and his sons were soon canvassing the area looking for carpentry and related work. Word of how nicely they had repaired their own home soon spread, and based on that projects success, and their growing reputation for quality work at a fair price with the work completed in a timely manner, Mac and Sons—as their booming business came to be known—were always busy.

As if they weren't busy enough, a land speculator was surveying the area in the hills overlooking the valley and also those hills that continued upward past the grove on the bluff. That speculator was looking to purchase as much of the land as he could and sell it off in parcels that could be bought by folks looking to own their own property and build a home on it. There was a reliable road that was well travelled by vehicles all day, every day. The road led to other communities, and all along its length, there were businesses of every size and type from small shops to actual factories. Jobs were plentiful, and people wanted to move into the area. The biggest obstacle to incredible, further development was a lack of suitable housing. Enter Mac and Sons, homebuilders and fine carpentry work.

Mac and Sons was their unofficial "company" name, and the fellow surveying the land had certainly heard of them. That man, an ambitious gentleman who smoked big cigars and whose name was Joe Massey, made plans to drop in on the MacKelvey family at the end of the day, and just as he was finishing up his surveying work, he observed the family men arriving home for supper.

Over the family supper, which he was cordially invited to share, Mr. Massey gave a detailed explanation of his ideas for the development of the slopes up behind their home. As they spoke, one of the boys noted that these plans truly were regarding the property *behind* their house. A hushed silence fell momentarily as everyone was mentally picturing the layout of their property. Indeed, the "back" of the house faced Hughes Street, and the traditional *front* of the house was about twenty yards from the edge of the bluff overlooking Rural Ridge Road and its community. No one at that dinner table actually said *"Hmmm"* out loud, but they were all certainly thinking it. Every MacKelvey, from dad to the youngest lad, knew at that moment that there house was actually facing the wrong way. But since it was the only house on that street or anywhere else on the bluff and surrounding hills, how could this be proven? Was it a mistake? What were the original builders thinking? So many questions and absolutely no answers.

Well, all that aside, here at their table in their new home that they'd lived in less than a year, was an opportunity of a lifetime for these brand new Americans. Oh, you thought they were Irish? Well, it's true they emigrated from Ireland, but everyone in the family had been sworn in as American citizens while in processing on Ellis Island in New York Harbor. Don't doubt for a moment that these good people weren't proud as peacocks about their Gaelic heritage, but they were now United States citizens and as proud of that as anything else.

Yes, indeed, laid out before them by Mr. Massey was a dream that these new Americans could be an integral part of, building quality houses for those eager to live in this area. Furthermore, there had been absolutely no development or building *behind* the house at No. 1 Hughes Street. It stood as a solitary sentinel overlooking the Rural Ridge Road and community with nothing behind but hills, woods, and potential. That would change dramatically beginning the next year early in the spring of 1921. In fact, there would be a few more subtle changes in the area, including the name of the community being created.

After dessert was served and the adults were talking business, without being missed or even noticed the youngest MacKelvey, a quiet but attentive child named Thomas Andrew slipped out of his chair and eased on out the back door quiet as you please. This youngster, who by virtue of his initials was Tam to everyone who knew him, wasn't interested in the conversation, nor fascinated by their dinner guest, and after all, he had finished eating. It was a nice warm spring early evening, and the boy felt like climbing in some trees.

His new yard wasn't the grove it had once been, but it still had quite a few trees that were excellent for climbing. The family had lived in a tiny house in the city back in Ireland, and Tam was completely enthralled by the large yard and the impressive number of fine old, totally climbable trees now available to him.

Hearing the screen door squeak open and then close, he turned around to see his sister, Katie, coming out of the house and walking toward him. Katie was only one year older than Tam almost to the day. Tam's birthday was October 3, and Katie's was one year earlier on October 5. They were the same size at this time, but Katie was the elder, and she gently, but willfully enforced her authority over him because of it. Tam really didn't mind it though, and in fact, the two siblings were pretty close companions, and after all, she simply wanted to climb a tree or two herself.

Tam and Katie, being the youngest MacKelveys, did not enjoy a scot-free life despite being the babies in the family. They had chores and responsibilities that by this time, they'd been doing for three and four years already. But they didn't have to leave the yard or the house if they didn't want to. The older kids all had to work outside of the family property and on it if it was called for, performing routine maintenance and other such tasks. Tam and Katie spent their free time climbing in and investigating every tree it was possible to do so. It should come as no surprise that they both agreed the big old sycamore was the very best tree, but they felt lucky to have such a nice yard with so many other excellent trees as well.

The old sycamore soon came to be the subject of a serious matter. Mr. Massey wanted the MacKelveys to build a barn like structure on their property that everyone working to build the new homesteads could keep their equipment in. Off to the edge of the property seemed the logical place. Just cut down that old sycamore, and there would be plenty of space to build a storage facility as big as was needed. Without much fanfare and precious little discussion, it was decided. Tomorrow, they'd cut down the big old sycamore and have its wood milled and use it to build that barn.

Ten-year- old Maggie MacKelvey, one of the two kids deemed the middle children, had overheard the plans being made for that old tree. Although she was a little too demure to be climbing trees, she had seen Tam and Katie doing so, and she saw the joy it brought them. Furthermore, that particular tree stood out in a big yard full of trees. It was *the* tree that everyone took notice of, and at that moment, only this young girl stood between it and the men with axes, in reality and metaphorically speaking.

Maggie went up and quietly told her younger siblings of the situation. Calmly and together, they talked the matter over, trying to think of alternate sites for the barn. Despite being children, they had grown up in a very responsible household. There was much love, but it was a practical household not given to too much sentiment or frivolous ideas. In other words, there was no waste, and the wants and needs of the individual was subordinate to the collective good of the entire family. They all really needed to talk to their dad and explain how much the tree meant to them.

It was dark when Mr. Massey climbed up onto his surveyor's wagon and headed to his hotel. He was staying in town rather than riding to and from his home in Pittsburgh. Because it was dark, the children's case for saving the tree was a bit more difficult to present. But in the course of their argument, their dad was mentally transported back in time to his own childhood home. That was a small farm in County Down some fifteen miles from Dublin. Small though it was, it had some of the finest apple trees in Northern Ireland, and oh, how he loved climbing in those. It was pure joy, and he never minded picking the apples either. Mac remembered with fondness that as a young lad, he had simply loved those trees.

The next morning, Mac was up and about right at dawn as was his custom. At first light, he took his coffee cup and walked out to the old sycamore. He was surprised he'd never noticed before just how perfect it was, and he was also thinking on how old this tree might be. Mac looked hard at the yard he had to work within, and it was going to be close. By that, it was meant that almost anywhere the barn was selected to be placed, it would most likely require cutting down at least one tree.

In the end, Mac configured a location fairly close to the original site, but this new spot didn't require any trees to be cut down. This resolution created the only problem that needed to be dealt with now, there would no longer be a free source of wood.

Coming up the road to continue surveying was Mr. Massey, already working one of those fat cigars he preferred. Mac hailed him, and over breakfast, he explained the situation to Mr. Massey. Smiling easily, the surveyor offered to rent the barn and its space for the duration of the building of new homes. and hopefully that would be several years. And by rent, he meant that he would supply the lumber while Mac and his boys with help from some of Massey's men would build the barn. Well now, sir. *That* was a plan! Mac and the boys weren't going to have to labor cutting down the tree, haul it to the lumberyard, and after it was processed, haul it back. Then, the fellows would have had to build that barn themselves. This way, they got help, the wood required for construction was free, there would be no big job cutting the tree down, and after it was all said and done, after the homes were built, Mac would have himself a fine, big barn.

Work commenced sooner than expected because there were more helping hands, and part of the work had been bypassed. Once the wood was delivered, the construction began. Five days later, when they were finished, it was a proper barn and generously shaded by the protective branches of that venerable old sycamore tree.

In the meantime, while construction was in progress, the younger siblings couldn't climb the sycamore, but they were pretty much free to squirrel up any other tree they pleased. Tam and Katie both chose a nice sturdy elm tree that, when they got as high into it as they could, their view was actually looking down toward the construction going on. Mama Mac made everyone stop working and come eat a lunch she and Maggie had spent all morning preparing. Prior to this lunch break, outside the house there was the constant sound of ringing hammers striking nails, saws singing through wood and the particular smell of all that cut wood. Inside, there was a flurry of activity as mom and daughter worked together in near perfect union to roast three chickens, peel, and boil ten pounds of potatoes, boil a couple of dozen ears of corn, and make several gallons of iced tea. Unfortunately, all there was for dessert were four freshly baked blueberry pies, but certainly no one was complaining. All of the fellows who had come by to help were advised that they didn't have to bring their own lunches the next few days, and that announcement was met with a round of cheers from the appreciative laborers.

The night that the barn was finished, the youngest siblings were quick to get right up into that old sycamore. The kids were thrilled that *they* had saved this tree; in fact, no trees were cut down. But the sycamore was hardly expected to know how close it had been to becoming something else on another part of the yard.

As soon as it was practicable, work started on building houses on each of the lots Mr. Massey had surveyed and started selling. Only the parcels of land sold were to see any construction. So, as soon as each house was finished, the family that had bought it moved right in. Almost every new family in what was truly becoming a neighborhood, either had children or was planning to have them. So, there were several new friends for the MacKelvey kids to play with. Because of this development, Tam and Katie spent very little time climbing the trees. In fact, they pretty much gave it up completely for doing other things with their friends. However, with very little, if any ceremony, their older sister, Maggie—the demure, stay-in-the-house kind of girl—had begun regularly visiting the sycamore.

It began innocently enough. One day, less than a week after it was finished, Maggie had strolled out to look at the new barn. Taking it all in, she noticed a flash of color up in the sycamore. It was too early for the leaves to turn colors, so she eliminated that possibility. Straining to see but not quite able to discern what the object was, she made a very uncharacteristic decision. Maggie slipped off her shoes and socks and began climbing up into that old tree toward whatever it was she had spotted.

The climb was easy, and in a few moments, she was holding a handkerchief that one of the workers must have dropped, and somehow the wind lifted it up and into that tree. Maggie put the cloth into her dress pocket and steadying herself by holding a branch, she began to survey her new surroundings.

Her first thought was that she was surprised she could stand up so easily without hitting her head. Her second thought was that to fall from here meant that you would certainly break at least one bone if not break your neck. That should have been a scary and discouraging thought to this domestic child, but it was not. Rather, she looked around further and noticed a particularly intriguing branch.

Maggie had to do some maneuvering and ducking under and stepping over several limbs, but she easily got to that attention-grabbing branch. Checking it out really close up, the girl thought to herself that it looked just like a seat. Working her way carefully onto the branch, Maggie got herself in position and gently sat down, resting her back against the thick tree trunk. It *was* a seat!

Over the next eight years, Maggie lost count of how many times she visited the tree. Like others who would follow in her attraction to that tree, to that special spot to just sit and be free, Maggie often took a book or brought something to eat.

On those hills, *behind* No. 1 Hughes Street, there were now other, newer roads leading to the several housing developments that had sprung up that were not only thriving but still growing, with new houses being built on demand. There were even houses being built on Hughes Street. But for the MacKelvey clan, their house and address would always be No. 1.

Part 12

Shared Interests, Oliver, and Aunt Mary

Oliver was feeling a little overwhelmed climbing down from his perch that evening. The sycamore has related so much information, and he'd never really thought about someone else living in their house, his family's house, *his* house. It was very cool to him, trying to imagine the area when theirs was the only house atop the bluff. Uncle Dave and Aunt Mary were watching television when Oliver went into the house, but Kathleen needed to be picked up from work at the hospital in Wolf Chapel, and Uncle Dave was going to get her. Oliver politely declined the invitation to go for that particular ride, he'd really prefer stay home to ask Aunt Mary about whomever lived in their house before her family. Besides, the round trip to fetch Kathleen home from work was invariably tedious, and there was always a lot of traffic.

With it being just the two of them, Aunt Mary fixed herself and Oliver ice cream sundaes. Together, they sat at the big, old dining room table and Aunt Mary, not knowing Oliver wanted to talk, started to do a word puzzle from her book of puzzles as she enjoyed eating of her sundae.

Not dissuaded in the least, Oliver pitched right in and asked his aunt who had lived there before her family. As they were both eating, Aunt Mary replied that she only knew a little bit about them, and that they had lived in the house through the Great Depression. Apparently afterward, or maybe even during the Depression the family, like many others, just seemed to fell on hard times and, she had heard that there were deaths in that family too. Aunt Mary told Oliver she thought that one or two of them might still be alive, but it had been years ago that they had all moved to various places, far away out of state. At any rate, she went on, that's what she had always heard, and she had no idea whether they ever visited the area again.

Aunt Mary knew quite well that Oliver spent his rare free time up in the tree as often as he could. She liked the way he was when he came down from being up in the branches awhile. He would be excited but in control. He asked excellent and interesting questions. Maybe best of all was the exercise in quality interaction between them that almost always ensued.

After a delicious sundae and excellent conversation, Oliver bid his aunt good night, put his dish and spoon in the kitchen sink, and was off upstairs to complete his bed time ritual of taking a shower if he needed one, brushing his teeth, saying his prayers, and maybe reading something before finally nodding off for the night.

Aunt Mary had always been interested in the local history and had quite a collection of old newspapers, news clippings, event mementos, photos, and more. She had been especially interested in the history of coal mining in that area, and the day Oliver had broached that very topic at the supper table, something akin to a distant memory sort of clicked—but nothing came of the feeling. It was just a weird twitch or something. She thought to herself, all that mysterious feelings nonsense aside, Oliver was becoming a joy to the point that the whole household wondered how they ever got along without him. Really.

She finished her sundae, put her dish and spoon in the sink, and went upstairs into the room that had long ago been set aside as a study. In that neat old room were several bookshelves, completely filled. There was an old desk with a new desktop computer and drawers where important family documents and papers were kept. Any wall space was covered by something framed and hung up—diplomas, family photos, and a really old photo taken from the back of the house looking way up to the woods toward the summit of the hills behind their house.

But Aunt Mary was looking for a book, a particular book entitled, *Bucket of Blood, The Ragman's War*, about those horrific mining company days of violence. Once she found it, she knew at a fleeting, remembering glance that it was probably too much reading for a seventh grader, even a bright and curious seventh grader like Oliver. But she thought to herself, reading it again would not only be good for her own intellectual stimulation, but help her to really fill Oliver in on that awful period in local history as well. As she turned out the light to leave the room, she glanced out the side window just in time to see a nearly full moon rising up over top of that old sycamore. It was a sight that brought an involuntary smile to Aunt Mary's face.

Soon enough, Oliver was heading back to school. His baseball team did a little better this year winning eleven games compared to nine last season. He had gotten amazingly better at competitive swimming, and his piano lessons were making some progress, but it was still rather painful to hear him practice. Time for climbing in the tree for the year was running out and fall weather was quickly taking over.

It was a late September, and the days were a little cooler, and the nights required a sweater or hoody. It was getting dark earlier too. In school, the history class was beginning to discuss the Great Depression. Oliver recalled from his last session with the sycamore that the Great Depression had adversely affected the MacKelvey family who were living in his house at that time. After supper and quickly getting his homework done, Oliver headed out to the great old tree. Maybe Oliver was used to it, or maybe he himself was getting bigger, but the tree wasn't as imposing to him as it once was. To be sure, the tree was definitely formidable, but Oliver seemingly never was intimidated or afraid to climb it. He never had been after the first time, but the tree just didn't seem as huge as it once did even though it *was* massive.

Climbing swiftly up and settling into his position, there was that initial, almost magical moment when the spirits of both of these living things, this old, old tree and this young boy, melded so smoothly and completely. It was a marvelous feeling. Oliver was paying keen attention as the story of the MacKelvey family during the Great Depression unfolded.

It was the year 1929, and there had been signs of financial trouble a couple of years prior when work slowed considerably. People weren't building or buying homes, jobs were scarce, and money was extremely tight. This wasn't just in America but was a situation repeated in country after country, around the world.

The MacKelveys were particularly hard hit because there were so many mouths to feed in that family. Bills, debts, and the costs of everyday living don't go away just because times are tough. It was a time of hardship and hard decisions. The eldest MacKelvey son, James, and his twin brothers, Matthew and Michael, had gone to Pittsburgh and enlisted. James had always had a rough and tumble side to his personality and apparently he joined the United States Marine Corps because it was allegedly the toughest branch of American military service. He never really felt a need to broadcast either his intentions or reasons, but in March of 1929, at the age of twenty-four, off he went to basic training at the Marine Corps Recruit Depot Parris Island, South Carolina.

The MacKelvey twins, Matthew and Michael, waited a few weeks for their mother to get over the shock and sadness of their older sibling going off to join the military before announcing their own plans. They had been plotting and planning to join the service for quite some time, but they kept it their secret, and once they saw how the family reacted to James signing up, they mutually agreed to wait a little while before springing another shock on the folks, and family in general. Then, one Sunday evening, in the late stages of the summer of 1929, as supper was being finished, the twins spilled the beans and revealed to everyone at the table that they too had gone to Pittsburgh and enlisted.

Their father looked long and hard at both of his boys, now sturdy young men, and without saying a word, simply got up and left the table. Their mother was fighting off tears and had a difficult time even forming the words to ask questions. Finally, she was able to articulate a simple one word query, "Why?"

Before the twins could answer, she followed up with two more quick inquiries, "Which branch, and when will you leave?"

Matthew had been born several minutes before his brother, so all their lives he had assumed the role as lead spokesman for both of them. He explained that they had joined the United States Navy, and they were going to the Great Lakes Naval Training Station somewhere north of Chicago, Illinois. They would be leaving home just after New Year's Day 1930.

It was on October 29, 1929, a day ever after referred to as Black Tuesday that the stock market crashed, plummeting not only the poor countries but the rich nations as well into economic and social upheaval. People living in cities, as well as those in rural areas, all suffered terribly. Earning money on a regular basis was nigh impossible, jobs all but nonexistent, and this widespread misery went on for four years in the United States. In some countries, recovery didn't begin until World War II, a full ten years later.

Christmas that year was especially memorable, and not for the presents everyone received, because if it weren't for James, there would have been no presents; it would have been all the family could do just to make a decent holiday meal. No, this Christmas was special because James, now a member of the Marine detachment aboard the battleship USS Texas, was home on leave through the holidays. James had not only been sending money home regularly the past nine months, but he had also been saving most of what he kept to himself. As a result, when James arrived home, he had brought with him a great big Christmas ham and fresh fruit and vegetables that would make a fine family feast. He also brought something special for each member of his family—these were souvenirs he'd picked up at various ports of call. Since he'd been assigned to the Texas, that ship had sailed to such exotic places as the Caribbean and through the Panama Canal to the Pacific Ocean and the Hawaiian Islands and back to the west coast of the United States before returning to the Atlantic Ocean and New York for an overhaul.

Mac, as the family patriarch, had long since come to accept that his twin sons were old enough to make their own choices, and he also knew that staying home would have been a titanic struggle since the onset of the Great Depression. However, James wasn't quite as diplomatic, and his concerns were of a different nature. He was concerned about who would help out around the family household and property.

When Mac explained how he'd come to grips with his own misgivings regarding the twins' enlistment, there was little choice for James to do anything less than hug his younger brothers and dad, long and hard. When they all let go, and there were four smiles to be seen through misty Gaelic eyes, James looked around making certain it was just the men in that room, and pulled a final gift out of his sea bag—a bottle of Irish whiskey. What made this particular gift so special and secretive was that Prohibition had been in effect since 1920, and aside from the "moonshine" available, there was no alcohol being consumed at all, and Mac, who dearly loved an occasional "taste," prudently never trusted anyone else's "shine." James gave the bottle to his dad who opened it and poured four small glasses while all were regaled with the tale of how James had bartered for that bottle with a British sailor. Yes, indeed, despite the Great Depression being upon the country and its adverse effects, this had been a very good and blessed Christmas at No. 1 Hughes Street.

Some time just after New Year's Day, the twins packed whatever the Navy had told them to bring, and they boarded the train for Pittsburgh. From there, they would catch another train to Chicago and go on to their training base. Both of them had done very well on the written examination given to all enlistees, and as a result, they were eligible for any enlisted job the Navy offered. Matthew opted for a job as a radio operator while Michael had decided on becoming a gunner's mate. They had made it a point to secure permission prior to signing any papers that regardless of what their jobs were, even if they were completely different, the twins would always serve together. Mac and James went as far as Pittsburgh on the train and saw the brothers off before returning home.

Both of the boys knew that James sent money home *and* was able to set some aside as well. During their time together that holiday season, James had told them how easy it was to save money while the ship was at sea. Naturally, it was more difficult whenever the ship was in some exotic, far away port, and there were distractions afoot and interesting and unique things to be bought. They promised him that they would endeavor to do no less when they started getting paid on a regular basis.

Back at the house at No. 1 Hughes Street, the mood was somewhat somber, but the younger MacKelvey kids loved having their big brother home from the Marines. They listened with rapt awe as he told them how big his ship was. He showed a postcard that he'd meant to mail from some European port but had forgotten to. It was a photo of the ship taken from an airplane flying overhead and was clear enough that anyone looking at it could easily see the individual sailor's on deck. That alone was awe-inspiring, to plainly see how huge that battleship really was. James went on to describe rough seas with gigantic waves crashing over the deck while they patrolled the North Atlantic. That tale was followed by his description of the passage through the Panama Canal, coming *and* going. Tropical Hawaii sounded too good to be true, and his vivid descriptions of San Francisco and other ports in California with warm sunshine all day, nearly every day, were especially appealing on those cold, snowy January days in 1930.

It was just a short week later when James had to pack up and say goodbye to his folks once more. He took the train to Pittsburgh alone, so his dad wouldn't have to ride back by himself. And just like that, the house seemed empty. All the older boys with their big voices were gone. Gone off to serve their adopted country.

A few months after James had left, on an early spring day, there came a knock on the back door. When Mama Mac answered, she saw a hobo, a homeless and displaced person, very dirty and disheveled asking for something to eat. Times were hard, but Mama Mac was a kindly woman accustomed to fastidious cleanliness about her home and her family.

Initially repulsed by the grimy creature standing before her, she directed him over to the barn. Gathering up some of Mac's old pants and a shirt, some soap, a large towel, and a bucket of hot water. she headed out to the barn and opening the door, she let the man inside. She instructed him to wash as thoroughly as was humanly possible given the circumstances, and when he was done, he was to change clothes and bring his dirty garb to her to be washed. She then left him and returned to the house to make him something to eat.

When the hobo reappeared at her back door holding out his filthy clothes for Mama to take, once again, she could only look at him and cringe, but she quickly composed herself. Cleaned up, he looked presentable enough, and she looked away from his face to the filthy clothes and told him that a change in plans dictated those must be burned. When he balked at that notion pleading that they were all the clothes he owned in the world, she kindly explained that she had a husband and three grown sons who had older clothes that he could wear.

Soon, the kids were coming home from school. As they were coming down the road, they saw the homeless fellow out in the yard talking with their mother. They walked up and were introduced to Zeke, as the fellow, whose real name was Ezekiel, preferred to be called. Mama Mac directed Zeke to go put his dirty old clothes over on the pile that would soon make a nice bonfire and get rid of some trash. As Zeke was doing so, Mac arrived home from an appointment, driven in a car by old Mr. Massey. As Mac made his way up the yard to the house, Zeke called out and explained his presence. Upon hearing that, Mama Mac came out to greet her husband and explain this unusual scenario.

Although it was a difficult time, the MacKelveys were known for their generosity and kindness, and besides, that family had been almost destitute at one time before, back in Ireland. Zeke was going to be welcome to whatever the family could give him, and that included a place to stay for a couple of days and nights. It has often been said that the road to Hades is paved with good intentions, and that time worn old adage would prove to be horribly accurate that very night.

Despite being kindly, the MacKelveys were practical and watchful. They had seen other displaced fellows since before the Great Depression had even started. These unfortunates were known as hoboes or bums or as some called them, tramps, men who rode the rail cars from town to town, sneaking aboard empty cars or loaded freight cars if they could gain entry and hide in them. They weren't necessarily bad people, but the depths of almost universal hardship that was cast over the country in those years turned even good people bad at times.

Zeke was one of those fellows. He was a good man at heart, but these hard times had made him desperate, not really a bad man, but not the honest, upright fellow he was before these stressful times hit the country. Mac told him he could sleep in the barn but only for two nights after which he had to be on his way. Zeke thanked him sincerely, and later, after supper, he headed out to the barn with a blanket borrowed from the house.

Sometime after midnight, Mac and Mama Mac were awakened to strange sounds coming from outside and there was an unusual glow as well. Both leapt from their bed and dashed to the window. The barn was in flames that had apparently started at the front and were quickly moving to the back of the structure.

Heat from the flames was curling and killing the tender new leaves just opening on that venerable old sycamore. The barn was going to be a total loss with the effort now to be concentrated on keeping the flames from spreading. Neighbors were out in their nightclothes with more people running toward the barn carrying buckets of water. The Rural Ridge Fire Department was soon on the scene, and their modern new equipment made certain that the flames were extinguished before causing further damage elsewhere.

The sycamore had received some heat damage, but the actual flames had been subdued before it was burned or even scarred very badly. But there was the question of what had started the fire, and where was Zeke? Mac told the assembled crowd that a hobo had been sleeping in the barn, and he wasn't anywhere to be found. As the charred wood was pulled away, a horrific spectacle was revealed. The dead and blackened body of the hobo was revealed, and in his fingers, frozen in a death grip, was the remains of a cigar. Nobody thought of it at the time, in fact only one person knew that as he was dropping Mac off at the house, Mr. Massey had tossed a less than half smoked cigar away. Zeke had seen this and his keen eye for something free had caused him to go fetch it when no one was looking. Somehow smoking that discarded cigar in the barn had ignited the hay or whatever and the flames had quickly spread. No one would ever know why he couldn't get out or somehow save himself, but none of that really mattered now. In the next few days, all the burned wood and things from inside the barn that were wrecked in the fire were cleaned up and hauled away. All that was left was the charred black outline of where the barn had stood, that and some slight heat damage to the otherwise intact sycamore tree.

A couple of years later, Maggie MacKelvey got married and went to live in California with her new husband. The middle child, Timothy, was in his early twenties and had secured a good job working on the railroad. He stayed with a traveling work crew and wasn't home often at nights. This left the young ones, Tam and Katie, as the only kids still at home. They were in school and spent their time studying or helping out around the house and yard. Their dad, Mac, had developed a bad back and was unable to work as hard as he was accustomed to. So, the kids picked up their dad's slack and everything possible got done under their mother's supervision.

It was just about 1933 and not an uneventful time in the MacKelvey household. The older boys had reenlisted, all three of them, and it looked like they would make careers of being in the military. Timothy had been promoted, sent to school, and had become an engineer with the railroad. Soon enough, his job necessitated a relocation out to the western states, and he eventually moved to Montana, settled there, and started a family. Mac, that hard working fellow who had kept his clan together before and after emigrating overseas, starting a whole new life and career watching his family grow and become independent young Americans and establishing his good name in his new homeland by employing those time tested virtues of honesty and quality workmanship. That strong willed Irishman who had persevered through everything, including the Great Depression, just never woke up one day. The doctor, who examined the body, claimed he had passed away in his sleep of a major heart attack. The family buried him in the Catholic Cemetery overlooking the Allegheny River the day before Thanksgiving of 1932.

After a rather bleak Christmas in 1932, in March of 1933, Mama Mac packed up the two youngest children and bought one way tickets to California. Maggie was unable to get home for her father's funeral, but she could easily envision what was happening back home. She wrote all of her brothers, none of whom were able to get back in time for the funeral either, and asked for their thoughts on this unfortunate development. Within a couple of months, the older kids had all agreed that their mother should sell the house and move to California with Maggie and her family. So they loaded up the truck, and they moved to Beverly Hills—that is, swimming pools and movie stars. And although they were fondly remembered for many years after by their former friends and neighbors, none of the MacKelvey family ever came back to Rural Ridge again. The great house at No. 1 Hughes Street was empty once again, but also once again, it wouldn't stay that way for long.

Part 13

Oliver's Times with Uncle Dave

Oliver knew more about those people from his house's past than he ever would have considered. It was a funny thing, he pondered, you really don't think much on those who might have lived in your house before you, but they were people, they had lives, and things happened to them in the house, out on the property, and in the neighborhood. He wondered if there were any pictures of these folks. There were other, older neighbors who had lived here longer than anyone else, and those people liked to meet occasionally at The Ravens Club. Oliver knew that because Uncle Dave and he used to eat lunch there, and he'd seen them, talking, showing each other pictures and such. Aunt Mary would know about any pictures, and she had known those same old timers since she was a kid.

Oliver was doing exceptionally well in American history, and once again, Aunt Mary was feeling especially close to the young lad. They had a shared interest in local history and spent quite a bit of quality time looking over her collection of papers, photos, and other related items. She was so pleased with the good, thoughtful questions he asked and whether by design or just sheer luck, he never let on where he got so curious. Together, they researched at the local library and found articles from back in the days when the MacKelvey family was making a name for themselves in the area building quality houses. All Oliver had to do was look around, down the street, and up on the hill to see well over forty houses that Mac and Sons had built before the Great Depression. There were also news clippings about the First World War, the mining violence, and lots of photos of the men, older and younger that had gone off to serve in the various conflicts the nation had been in over the past hundred years or so, including the MacKelvey boys. Oliver was also very interested in hearing what Aunt Mary had to say about when her family moved to this house and what it was like for her growing up in this area forty years ago or so.

Autumn was soon there in all its color and splendor, not to mention all the chores and work associated with that season. Oliver had just celebrated his twelfth birthday, Uncle Dave had mowed the yard for the last time, and the first Saturday afternoon spent raking leaves and gathering up sycamore balls was looming on the horizon. The sycamore seemed to have outdone himself this year by the look of all the yellow leaves practically heaped in a circle around its area, and it still had quite a few to drop yet.

That Saturday did roll around quickly, and immediately after a great big, special weekend breakfast, the fellows headed out to the garage to fetch the rakes, big, black plastic garbage bags for the leaves and the big drop cloth used to gather up the sycamore balls. Oliver and Uncle Dave were out in the yard earlier than usual because it was the first day, and there was quite a bit to do. Furthermore, they were both eager to get the job done so that they could watch college football. These two pals loved watching college football together, snacking on chips and dip and cool drinks. They particularly loved watching their favorite team, the University of Pittsburgh Panthers, aka Pitt. That was the team playing on prime time television that day versus in-state rival, Penn State. It should go without saying, given where they lived that they were naturally diehard Pittsburgh Steeler fans as well.

So, knowing what a good time was to come later and with that goal in mind, the two set to work raking the leaves into big piles and then stuffing them into those sturdy black, plastic garbage bags. Those bags, once filled to capacity and tied up at the top, were then toted down to the bottom of the driveway and left by the mailbox that was roadside. Rural Heights is what the community was now called after originally being known as Rural Ridge. After the flurry of homes being built up on the hill behind the bluff, and No. 1 Hughes Street pretty much ended, the locals almost naturally began referring to the area as "The Heights," and the community voted one year to change the name of their community, albeit only slightly.

Several times, every fall, the village of Rural Heights would drive around with a big dump truck and collect those bags to be taken to the large community mulch pile behind the community Department of Public Works, or DPW building. That building was also the fire station, police station, mayor's office, tax collector's office, and council meeting place. You could vote there too. The sycamore balls stayed on the property though as they were tossed on Uncle Dave's personal mulch pile in the upper corner of the property right by the edge of the bluff. Tossing those balls meant the end of a job well done that would immediately be celebrated by putting the tools away and getting two cans of ice cold root beer to satisfy their justified thirsts. But we're getting ahead of ourselves.

Later in the morning, when the two hard working yardmen were hauling those bags to the curb, a car with four very dignified older ladies pulled up and stopped beside them. The driver rolled down her window and asked Uncle Dave if he were the property owner, and when he acknowledged that he was, she began asking about a few of his trees, the sycamore in particular. The other ladies, who, up to this point had been silent, became very animated and started chattering in their effusive gushing over that grand old tree. And that was the very point of their combined inquest and visit; that old sycamore in Uncle Dave's yard had been reported to their group as quite possibly being somewhat historic given its age and size.

Uncle Dave directed the ladies to park their car where they were and accompany him up to examine the tree they believed might be of important historical significance. They continued chattering at each other as they exited the automobile and began ascending the long driveway. Of course, they might have driven up the driveway and parked on the pad, saving them a rather tasking walk. However, Uncle Dave had to discourage anyone from driving up because inevitably, when it came time to leave, the following would occur. In backing up and getting turned around, cars would drive onto the grass and leave tire marks in the yard. This was unacceptable to Uncle Dave, and when it was damp or rainy, it exacerbated the problem. So, no, folks had to walk up the driveway to visit the house and property—unless it was their first visit—or there was no family member out in the yard to advise them where to park. Uncle Dave truly detested those times.

As the four ladies from the National Arbor Foundation, Greater Pittsburgh Area Chapter, came into the presence of the great tree, they were immediately silenced, one and all. Oliver thought he'd noticed their car earlier, slowly cruising past on a couple of occasions while he and his uncle worked in the yard, and now he realized that he had indeed. Their comments about espying the tree from afar and standing in its shadow were telling. There was no doubt in the boy's mind that these genteel grandma types *had* been casing the joint.

Once they got over their initial awe, these dear old ladies once again began chirping at each other and reaching into their respective purses. Oliver wondered to himself how the four could all speak simultaneously and understand each other, but they did. These arboreal enthusiasts were well prepared for the task of measuring, photographing, and taking copious notes regarding the wonderful specimen they were zealously examining so thoroughly.

When they were quite satisfied, they'd been as thorough as possible, the driver announced that her quartet unanimously agreed that this tree was indeed significant. They went on to state that quite likely it would be cited by the Arbor Foundation and declared a national living monument, a natural treasure. This would entail a handsome, permanent metal plaque being placed in the ground at the base of the tree, and that old sycamore would be listed on the national register of historic trees.

The ladies uttered their most sincere thanks to the family who, by this time, had all gathered in the yard to see what the fuss was all about, and began the long, almost equally arduous descent down the driveway to their car. After their visitors had gone, Aunt Mary felt a strange, unexplained bit of emotion as Uncle Dave and Oliver regaled her with the details of the entire encounter with the older tree ladies.

When everything settled down, and Aunt Mary and Kathleen had gone back into the house, Uncle Dave and Oliver dumped those sycamore balls and repaired to the garage and a tasty, ice cold root beer reward. Oliver told Uncle Dave how much he loved that old sycamore and how special he'd always believed it was without any affirmation from some outside source. A smiling Uncle Dave told Oliver he knew the tree was special to the boy, and at that very candid moment, Uncle Dave took the opportunity and revealed how proud he was of his nephew— his nephew who in less than a year would turn thirteen years old. Oh no! Those traditionally tumultuous teen years were about to happen at No. 1 Hughes Street . . . again.

After watching the Pitt-Penn State football game with the family, Oliver felt a familiar twinge. It wasn't necessarily a physical thing or something actually felt, but rather an urge. After supper, he was going to go hang out with and in the soon to be officially recognized as famous sycamore.

Conversation at that evening's meal was a bit livelier than usual, and the table talk in that house was rarely uninspired, especially lately. There was much speculation and proud recollections about the sycamore from Aunt Mary. She also vividly recalled the stories she had heard about her grandparent's reactions the first time they visited their potential new home.

Part 14

Meet the Rubinskys

A unt Mary's grandparents, Casper and Irene Rubinsky, were a young, newly married couple recently emigrated from Gdansk, Poland. Before leaving Poland, Casper's father and last living relative had passed away a couple of months earlier, and the seventeen-year-old son had inherited a small industrial factory making fittings for ships. Gdansk is Poland's chief seaport and the family business thrived, in fact, it was in real need of expansion. The building, the equipment, everything related to that particular business needed upgrading. Casper realized this, and despite growing up learning and working in the business, he had an insatiable desire to do something else. He also realized that his disinterest and possible procrastination regarding the necessary improvements could easily lead to financial disaster and ruination.

So, seeking professional advice and being told that given his lack of interest, selling the business was the prudent thing to do, Casper advertised its availability. Within a month, he had gotten out of what he regarded as a boring business obligation and done so with a pocketful of money. He discussed future plans with his bride-to-be, Irene, who was also seventeen years of age, and the two decided to immediately get married and start their new lives together in America.

There was much discussion over where to establish their life together in America. It was, after all, a huge country area-wise compared to their native Poland. One evening, Irene told Casper that after thinking back on their discussions, it was clear to see that there were a few factors that were remarkably consistent in their talks. Chief among these details was that the couple obviously preferred living in the eastern United States. When California was mentioned, and Casper quashed that notion immediately with a dismissive wave of his hand, Irene was secretly pleased. Furthermore, their research had shown that there were several large Polish communities in a few American cities at that time. Pittsburgh was among those cities, and to really seal the deal, Pittsburgh had a neighborhood known as Polish Hill. So there it was; they hugged, laughed, and declared it was Pittsburgh for them.

So here in the early spring of 1933, Casper and Irene arrived in Pittsburgh as newly declared United States citizens and took a taxicab to Polish Hill to look for housing. They leased an apartment on a monthly basis in an affordable if not pristine building in that neighborhood. They had never even thought of looking anywhere else for housing, and that was somewhat regrettable because, though they had both grown up comfortably in the crowded harbor town of Gdansk, they now felt they wanted more space between their neighbors and themselves. That led the young couple to look out in what are now the suburbs for permanent housing, a home of their own with some property. A newly made friend, and fellow Polish émigré, had a car and drove them around the greater Pittsburgh area looking at prospective homes.

It would have been easy to miss the turn off onto Hughes Street, but something told Irene to request the driver turn up onto the next street they could. A few minutes later, the three of them were getting out of the vehicle and staring with great admiration at the large house before them that had a for sale sign in the yard by the road.

Walking over the vacant property, the couple noted several things, some ideas they shared, and some were just quietly noted personal observations. There was no driveway in those days per se, but there was still evidence of the pathway worn out by the trucks and wagons going back and forth from the now completely gone barn, down to Hughes Street. There was also the outline where the burnt down barn had once stood. Casper noted these things and was already forming a few ideas in his head for implementation after they bought this house.

Irene wrote down the real estate contact number, and the trio motored back to the city. She immediately called the real estate agent and arranged to meet him there to see the house inside and out. That night, the Rubinskys conversation was very excited and all about that great house, which they hadn't even seen the inside of yet. Without saying so and realizing all too well that he was putting the cart before the horse, as the saying goes, Casper knew in his heart that he wanted to buy that house. Irene was more candid and declared without hesitation that it was exactly the home and property of her dreams.

Their friend generously loaned the couple his car, and, next day, they all met at the house—the agent, and the prospective buyers. Immediately upon entering the front door that was in the back of the house, Irene was overwhelmingly impressed by the beautiful woodwork that was present in the entry way and, as the couple soon saw for themselves, all through the house as well. The young bride knew, without a doubt, that she wanted them to live there, but then, she had felt that way all along. After touring the house, the young couple heard the real estate agent give his standard speech and sales pitch, but that was all unnecessary, because these two happy, newly married, even newer American citizens, had found their dream house. This would be the place they started their family and would spend the rest of their lives, together.

On the way out, after shaking hands to seal the sale, Casper took Irene by the hand and led her over to this one particular tree. He was uncertain of its exact variety, but he admired its shape, size, and beauty. He had mentally evaluated all of the older and larger trees in the expansive yard, but this one stood out. Casper still held his wife's hand while he gestured with his free hand. He told her of his wish to pave a driveway leading up to the blackened base work of the old barn. He described in great detail his dream of building a garage big enough for the two cars he wanted to buy and that, coincidentally, was also the exact size of the barn.

After Casper and Irene bought the house at No. 1 Hughes Street, he had decided that he was going to turn one of his hobbies, photography, into his new profession. He set up a small studio in the basement and began advertising his new service with posters and word of mouth. He had a talent, and he was especially good at portraits. The couple had spent the bulk of their money on getting to America, becoming citizens, and they paid cash for the house, so although they were far from broke, it was imperative that Casper started earning again.

Almost two years later, with the happy couple comfortably established in their great new home, some of Casper's other dreams were coming to fruition. He had built the big garage as planned, and the proposed driveway was the next project to be completed. When that driveway was finished, Casper stood back looking on with a combination of pride and a puzzling sense of misgiving on what he'd achieved.

There should be no sense of misgiving, his wife admonished him, but yet there was something nagging away at his brain. He couldn't shake the feeling that there was to be something else, something that might turn out to be the proverbial crowning touch. But at the moment, whatever that something else might be, was completely eluding him.

That same night, long after the couple had retired to bed, Casper awoke with a start. He leapt out of bed and grabbed his bathrobe. In a later recounting of this story, his groggy and startled wife would liken his behavior at that moment to Archimedes having his "Eureka!" moment. Irene dutifully put on her slippers and nightrobe and followed Casper downstairs.

All he needed was a staff to be seen as Moses as he held out his arms widely and began gesturing toward the newly completed driveway before exclaiming. "Trees!" That was all he could say at first. He then began to be a little more articulate as he told his wife he would plant trees all along the length of the driveway from Hughes Street at the bottom almost to the garage itself. There were already a number of fine trees on the property, but Irene was beginning to see his vision and she suddenly blurted out, "Pine trees!"

Casper excitedly grabbed her and held her tight for a long moment, looking over his wife's shoulder as he imagined those trees were already in place, then they once again retired to the house and their warm bed. The very next day, he contracted for twelve eastern White Pine trees to be planted at specific intervals along the left side of the driveway going up. This allowed for growth both upward and outward although that particular genus of trees grows mostly upward, easily reaching heights of seventy-five to eighty feet and more. They grew relatively fast too, and, soon, they were a beautiful addition to an already fabulous yard.

Oliver's twelfth year had passed with a particular swiftness and he was soon to become a teenager. His athleticism continued to improve, he was a solid student, very good at some subjects, pretty good in others but thankfully not terrible in anything at all in his scholastic endeavors. While the previous year had melded into his life in a rather routine way, the changes in him were quite evident to those closest to the boy. He understood and accepted his mother's untimely passing and he was extremely appreciative of the life his Aunt Mary and Uncle Dave, now called Mom and Dad, had afforded him. He returned their kindness and generosity by being a good boy, a good kid that people liked and one that could be counted on. He was responsible and very loving and had become a most welcome addition to their little family. Yes, life and things in general were very good for young Oliver Logan. Why, even his new and occasional battles with acne were proving to be obstacles that he could overcome fairly easily. Life was good!

Oliver was thinking on all of this as he headed out to lounge up in the sycamore. He quickly settled into his spot, and that magic moment immediately transpired. The boy had no way of knowing but his tree, in a way only another arbor could ever understand was *feeling* some angst, a sense of urgency. Oliver's birthday was a mere two weeks away, and after that, once he was a teen, these moments would cease forever. There was still much to impart to the boy before that happened.

Innately sensing through Oliver approximately where Aunt Mary had left off, the sycamore continued the impartation by relating things that happened afterward. Casper and his wife had three children in the first five years they lived in the house, including the second set of twins to grow up there, and by New Year's Day of 1939, there was a lot of activity and commotion going on all the time.

The couple had birthdays only two months apart, so they were, more often than not, the same age in years even though Irene was technically the elder. Both were twenty-three years old and just a few months from turning twenty-four. As blissfully happy as they were with their domestic lives, several things were happening in Europe that didn't bode well for the continued peace there, and the Japanese were being extremely aggressive in the Far East and other Pan Asian areas as well.

Then the worst possible events occurred in Poland. On September 1, 1939 the German army attacked Poland by air and land in a combined arms tactic that became known as *blitzkrieg*, or lightning war. Meanwhile, that same morning, in the Polish city of Danzig, a "visiting" German battleship was moored in the harbor, and at dawn began shelling the city at point blank range effectively starting what became the European Theatre of World War II.

Casper and Irene were torn emotionally. While Casper had no really close family left in Poland, Irene had a lot of relatives now in harm's way. Together, they prayed for a bit of good news and even a miracle if possible. But the situation worsened, and by October, Poland had been not only been overrun and surrendered, but it had been divided up and claimed by both Germany and Russia. While they both continued to pray, Casper was also considering an alternative plan.

Growing up in Poland, Casper had lived a very comfortable life. The family wasn't rich by any means, but they did have more than most Polish citizens. This meant a better than average education and being able to indulge in hobbies and fantasies that people of less affluence were not. To that end, Casper's father had paid for him to receive flying lessons, and Casper quickly earned his pilot's certification papers. He hadn't done any flying since arriving in America, but the thrill of flying had always stayed with him.

All of the thoughts and emotion coursing through his brain was confusing. He had read that there were a large number of Polish air force pilots and personnel that had escaped to serve with the British who were now at war with Germany. Casper had even heard of a few Americans going off to fight with the RAF, the British Royal Air Force. However, he had also learned that because of rather strict "neutrality laws," American citizens were banned from serving another country in war time.

With a very distraught young wife and three young children, Casper was truly torn between patriotism and his overwhelming yen to be a good father and do the right things, whatever those might be. He weighed all the pros and cons and decided that he *must* go fight the hated Nazis, with or without Irene's or the American government's consent.

At that point, there was no question of Irene being for or against such a drastic move on his part because he hadn't even discussed it with her. But he finally did broach the subject, and surprisingly, she was rather acquiescent about the whole matter. It was almost as though his young wife had read his mind. She listened quietly while he explained his feelings and all that he'd learned about Americans and Poles flying and fighting with the RAF.

Together, they discussed every facet of this potential venture, and after doing so, they agreed to look further into the matter as a team. Through Polish friends they had met since arriving in the Pittsburgh area, contacts were made, inquiries posted, and by Halloween of 1940, Casper had surreptitiously been accepted by the RAF as a Polish volunteer. The day after Thanksgiving, in a tearful departure, he had hugged and kissed his young family goodbye, taken the train to Pittsburgh, then to New York City, on to Montreal, Canada, and finally Halifax, Nova Scotia. There, along with several young Canadians and a couple of other American lads who were both travelling under the same orders, he boarded an armed merchant vessel bound for England. Casper had all the necessary papers and documentation he was instructed to bring, very few personal possessions, and a very full heart. He felt proud of what he was about to undertake, and yet he would never get over being away from his beloved family.

Irene knew little or nothing about photography, and to be honest, she couldn't have cared less about it. From her perspective, the best thing about photography was that it made Casper happy, and he was earning a decent wage being a shutterbug.

He had made quite a few acquaintances in his profession, and people liked him and his family. That seemingly positive notoriety soon turned out to be a double-edged sword, however.

Because of the aforementioned neutrality laws and the fact that Casper was now an American citizen, his being gone all of a sudden became the subject of idle gossip. Soon enough, United States federal agents visited the house with a lot of questions that required answers. Irene was scared and deservedly so because these agents took unnecessary advantage of the young immigrant mother home alone with three children and threatened her with deportation if she were discovered to have lied as to her husband's whereabouts.

Keeping a cool head despite her overwhelming nervousness, she calmly told these agents that her husband had left her and the children. Yes, she knew not why, but he had just vanished one night. No note, no warning, he just up and disappeared. No, they hadn't discussed anything about him returning to Europe for revenge or any other motives. Yes, she told them, they were both quite distraught by what had happened in Poland and what was then happening elsewhere in Europe. But current events were all they had discussed, she told them, and she hadn't a clue why or where Casper had disappeared to. She somehow managed to convince these skeptical Feds of her innocence regarding this whole Casper disappearing business, and they left her with a strong admonishment to contact the federal government if he should return or if she heard from him. After they had gone, badly shaken by this menacing visit, Irene took the children out for a walk to calm down and think on their immediate future.

It was getting pretty dark by this time, and Oliver realized he ought to head back into the house. Once again, as he dropped down out of the sycamore and began walking toward the house, his young mind was racing with what he'd been "told" and what there was yet to be learned about the Rubinsky family. Once inside, he hung up his hoody and sought out his aunt, who was in the kitchen making herself some tea. As she began preparing him a cup of tea as well, Oliver told her he was seeking answers to a myriad of questions.

It was easy and seamless slipping right into a conversation with Aunt Mary about that family who lived in this very house so long ago. In fact, she told him, Casper Rubinsky was actually her grandfather!

Yes indeed! And she did know exactly what happened to them, in great detail at that. Casper had left for the war in late November of 1940, and a short year later, on December 7, 1941, the Japanese had staged a surprising sneak attack and bombed the US naval base at Pearl Harbor in Hawaii drawing America into another war the nation had striven to stay out of.

Since Casper had left his new home in America under clandestine circumstances, he was effectively unable to write home or in any other way communicate with his wife and children. Then, one day in early March of 1942, a young fellow had come by their house to secretly deliver a message that Casper entrusted him with. This man was a native Pittsburgher who had been studying in England when the war started. He would have returned to America much sooner, but he had met and fallen in love with an English girl and probably would have stayed there until whenever, except that America's entry into the war made him think differently.

This stranger had met Casper straight out of the blue when, perchance, the two happened to be in the same pub at the same time. Casper heard someone ordering pints of ale in an accent that made his ears prick up. He strained to catch more of that peculiar voice and accent. He located the source of the voice, and when the speaker turned and looked at him, Casper pointed at him, so there was no mistaking to whom he was speaking and asked, "Have you ever been to the Oyster House in downtown Pittsburgh?"

Surprised at first and completely taken aback, the stranger smiled and responded that he had indeed and followed that up with an affirmation that they had the best fish sandwiches around. Introductions were in order, and the expatriate Pittsburgher identified himself as Ronnie. After excusing himself from the group at the table where he had been sitting, Ronnie and Casper established themselves in new seats at the bar to talk.

This congenial fellow, Ronnie, whose surname has long since been forgotten if it was ever remembered in the first place, revealed to Casper that he'd had grown up in the Squirrel Hill area within walking distance of the University of Pittsburgh campus. After graduating from Pitt in the Class of 1938, he had matriculated to King's College in London to continue his studies. As affable as this fellow Pittsburgher was, Casper knew for a fact that London was rife with German spies, and for that reason alone, as much as he wanted to, he was loathe to trust anyone he didn't know, even this man with an undeniably Pittsburgh accent.

But the two continued to drink and chat about home (Pittsburgh) and agreed to meet the next day at the same pub at a specific time. Casper had explained that he was on a short military leave and had to catch his ride back to their airfield, a rendezvous that could not be waivered. Ronnie had logically presumed by the fact that Casper was in uniform that he was military, but did not pry or ask any awkward questions of his new acquaintance.

As agreed, they met at the appointed time at the same cozy pub the next day. Having thought long and hard about many aspects of his new associate, Casper formulated a few questions that if answered correctly would corroborate Ronnie's claims as well as put Casper's mind at ease over something he desperately wanted and needed to do.

During their initial meeting, Ronnie had told Casper that since America was now in the war, he was going to marry his British sweetheart and return to the States with her. Once there, he planned to have his new bride live in his childhood house with his parents and sisters who still lived at home. It was then his plan to enlist in the Army and serve his country.

Knowing Ronnie would be back in Pittsburgh long before he would, if indeed Casper would ever see his new homeland again, he resolved to task Ronnie with executing a highly personal favor. But first, he needed to know beyond the shadow of a doubt that Ronnie was trustworthy. He casually inserted pointed questions into their conversation. Seemingly harmless inquiries that Casper was familiar with that most likely only another Pittsburgh native could correctly answer.

After he was satisfied that Ronnie was legitimate, Casper pulled a small envelope from the pocket inside his jacket. He held it tightly as he began explaining what it was and what he had been doing in England since before America entered the war.

This was the first opportunity since he'd left home that Casper had to communicate with Irene and his children. They hadn't heard from him in well over a year, and of course, he hadn't heard from them since his whereabouts were a military secret. He went on to explain how he arrived in England and that he was now flying Spitfire fighter planes with a Polish unit attached to the RAF. His contract was for the duration of the war or until he was either injured too badly to be of further military service or killed. Casper told Ronnie that he had saved almost all of his pay since coming to England and desperately needed someone to secretly deliver that saved money along with several, long overdue letters, a photo of him in his uniform beside his plane and a lock of his hair.

He was misty-eyed as he handed the precious envelope to Ronnie, and it was with an almost equally heavy heart that Ronnie accepted this solemn assignment. In truth, there was absolutely no way Casper could know if Ronnie was truly a man of his word or not, but these were desperate times that often called for desperate measures. He handed the envelope to Ronnie and sat back, exhaling a heavy sigh.

Three months later, there was a knock on the back door of that big house at No. 1 Hughes Street. It was a young man in a military uniform, and the sight caused some degree of alarm in Irene. She opened the door slightly and listened as the young soldier told her the purpose of his visit. As soon as he mentioned that he was sent there by Casper, Irene practically flung the door open and dragged him inside.

She excitedly bade her now very welcome visitor to come sit down in the kitchen, and without asking if he was hungry, she began making him a sandwich and cup of coffee. While she was doing this, Ronnie told her the whole story of how he'd met her husband, and he patiently answered each of her questions to the best of his ability. As Irene set this modest repast on the table before him, he realized it was the perfect moment to relinquish responsibility for the envelope he'd brought from that tiny, crowded pub in London, and without another word, he pulled it from his pocket and handed it to her.

Ronnie ate in silence as he watched her hesitate to open it. She held it close to her heart for a long moment before holding it up and simply staring at it for a while, transfixed by the writing on the envelope that she recognized as her dear husband's penmanship. She smiled and held it up to her nose expectantly, but there was no single, really discernible scent. Irene looked at it one more long moment before using a butter knife to slice it open. She carefully withdrew the contents and placed them before her on the table. She saw the money, she saw the small piece of tissue paper containing a lock of her husband's hair, and she saw the black and white photo of that handsome young man standing there proudly in uniform beside his aircraft. But it was his letters that she was really interested in, and she opened one and began reading it with a longing and desperation only a woman, only a wife in her situation could appreciate. Through teary eyes, she looked up and across the table at this young man who had proven to be as faithful to his word and honor as another stranger could ever hope for.

There was a brief paragraph explaining how Casper had met Ronnie and come to entrust him with this sacred mission. Irene composed herself and introduced her three daughters who had gathered bashfully in the kitchen doorway. With his mission accomplished and having other obligations, Ronnie excused himself from their pleasant company, and just as suddenly as he had appeared, he was gone.

When Oliver pressed his aunt for more information about her grandparents, her usual cheery countenance took on a more somber look.

Sometime before Ronnie visited the house and delivered among other things, Casper's savings from England, Irene used her husband's positive local notoriety to offset the loss of his income as a photographer. This clever woman debated whether to seek work in the factories supporting the war effort as so many woman were doing with most of the men being drafted or enlisting, or try something else. That *something else* turned out to be the idea that with the men gone away, and the women working in their places at the factories, there was suddenly a great need for childcare in the community.

These workingwomen needed someone to watch over their children while they were working. The Rubinskys were a respected name in the neighborhood and had an impeccable reputation even with the mysterious disappearance of one Mr. Casper Rubinsky. Furthermore, Irene had a big house with a huge yard, and the area was safe. So, knowing she had her neighbors' trust, Irene put up flyers and notices announcing her availability and willingness to provide secure babysitting services to the local female workforce that needed her.

The task was to prove much more challenging than she ever thought it might be because every kid is different, and there were considerable age differences to be aware of. But there were never any unseemly incidents, no serious accidents, and never a shortage of clientele—who always paid with cash. All in all, her business thrived and kept her busy, but her thoughts often turned to Casper whom she missed fiercely, although she now knew there were only three conditions under which he could come home. The anguish of missing her husband was made worse by the fact that with the lone exception of the recently delivered and much cherished letters, she would not, more than likely, be hearing from Casper again any time soon.

By the fall of 1945, the bloodiest, most destructive war in human history had come to an end with the Allied forces universally victorious over their Axis foes in both the European and Pacific theatres. The war in Europe had ended in May, but the vicious and bloody conflict against Japan in the Pacific raged on until August. Wartime protocol was still in effect, even though the conflict was over and the troops were coming home in droves. The Rural Heights area had seen many of its menfolk serve in the war, but, thankfully, the area experienced precious few casualties or local men killed or wounded. While this was indeed a blessed thing, it marked a turning point in Irene's cottage industry business watching her neighbor's children while they worked. Fortunately, she was, by nature, a frugal, practical young woman and had managed to save quite a bit of her earnings, and Casper, with the money he sent her, had proven to be a wonderful provider from afar.

A year passed by, and there were celebrations hailing the first anniversary of VE (Victory in Europe) and VJ (Victory over Japan) Days. Another anniversary was soon to occur, a somber occasion that was becoming increasingly harder to bear for the four Rubinsky women. Yes, the three little girls that Casper had kissed goodbye seemingly so long ago were now quite grown. Not only were they six years older, but Olivia, now age twelve, and the twins, Cicely and Tarin, were eleven years old, and all three were quite mature for their ages. The war had that kind of effect on most of their generation's children, and conditions had necessitated that those kids were forced to grow up quickly and accept a lot of responsibility that most generations of children escape.

A few days after these celebrations ended, the Rural Heights postman rode his bicycle up the long driveway and over to the back door of the house. It was warm, and the doors were open with the screen doors now in use. His arrival was noticed as soon as he turned up the driveway, and the entire household was on the porch awaiting him expectedly because this was far from the normal mail delivery, in fact, in those days, there was no mail delivery. Routine dictated that someone go down to the post office every day to check for mail, and since folks rarely received much mail in those days, having it actually delivered right to your door was very out of the ordinary.

Irene accepted the letter being handed to her and signed the form as the postman directed her to. The girls all bid him farewell and thank you as he mounted his bicycle and rode away. A very distracted Irene was examining the envelope, carefully noting that it had passed through several official entities and three countries before arriving at the Rural Heights post office. There was actually a letter in an envelope contained within the outer envelope, and it too was littered with postmarks and official stamps.

As they retreated back inside, Irene was trembling as she slipped her finger under the seal and dragged it along the letters length to open it. She sat down as she withdrew an official missive from the RAF, and there was another one from the Polish government in exile in England as well.

Sighing heavily and mustering her strength, she began reading, fearfully expecting the worst. Despite long ago preparing to possibly one day hear the very worst possible news of her husband's fate, what she read was still a tremendous blow, and she sobbed uncontrollably. Her daughters flocked to her side, and she desperately hugged them all the while wondering how she could break this tragic news to them.

Their father was dead and had been for almost three years. Because of wartime protocol and the secrecy of his participation in spite of being an American citizen, it was decided by the powers that be to wait until war's end to release any information on those foreign volunteer pilots that were lost in combat. The Polish government's letter described his death and proclaimed him a hero. Witnesses who flew with him that fateful day in 1943 stated that he displayed uncommon valor and was one of the better pilots in the squadron.

The typical and most successful Polish fighter air combat tactic of the day called for a pilot to close in on an enemy plane, waiting until the last possible moment before opening up with their .50 caliber machine guns. It was at once a dangerous but highly effective tactic. Casper was executing that tactic when his plane was badly damaged by gunners aboard the German Heinkel-111 bomber he was attacking. Despite the severe damage to his own plane and having undoubtedly been wounded as evidenced by the testimony of others who observed the shattered acrylic bubble of the canopy of his cockpit, he flew under his original target and deliberately crashed his plane into the next, closest enemy bomber creating a horrific explosion with no survivors from either aircraft.

During all the time she had known Casper, Irene never doubted his sincerity or loyalty, and though there had previously been no opportunities for him to display any real valor, she sensed it was who he was at heart. She tearfully reflected on his decision to go fight the hated Germans, and now, at the saddest moment in her relatively young life, she was never prouder of him, nor had she ever loved him or missed him more.

Irene once again composed herself and sat the girls down on the big couch in the living room with her to tell them their father was never coming home again. As she was gathering herself to tell them, there was another knock at the door. Distressed at being bothered at such an inopportune time, she walked through the living room into the kitchen. It was the postman again, and he apologized as he handed her another official envelope also covered in stamps and postmarks. Never stopping to consider what bad news this might be, she almost absent-mindedly tore open the envelope and withdrew its contents.

When she looked over the document in her hands, she simply swooned, fainted dead away, and crumpled to the floor. Immediately, her daughters were about her gently tapping her cheeks and shaking her to bring her back to consciousness. Slowly, she came to, and as she sat up and accepted a cool glass of water, her mind was racing. In that envelope was a government cheque made out to her to the tune of [1]$15,000. Ten thousand dollars was the standard governmental pay-out in soldier's life insurance, the rest was a combination of Casper's combat pay, bonuses he received for each enemy plane he shot down, and an additional handsome sum collected by his fellow fighter pilots in that Polish RAF squadron. Irene was now an emotional wreck, her heart torn asunder by absolute dismay compounded by conflicting elation as she revealed everything to her daughters.

Irene stayed at the house several years afterward, but eventually met someone, remarried, and early in 1954, moved away to Dubuque, Iowa, where she lived for the rest of her life. After using their new fortune prudently, she left almost everything to her girls who wanted to stay in the area and especially that house, despite their mother leaving.

---

[1] In case you are wondering, that sum of $15,000 in 1946 would be almost $200,000 in 2017 as one dollar in 1946 equals $13.27 at the time of this writing.

Part 15

A New Mistress at No. 1
Hughes Street

O livia Rubinsky, being the eldest daughter, assumed overall control of the house, but it was truly a democracy as each sister had an equal say in all important matters. They all lived prudent lives as learned from their extremely practical mother, and they kept the house in great shape through regular proper maintenance and a keen eye for necessary improvements. The twins matriculated to, and graduated from, the University of Pittsburgh, but their individual choices of major fields of study would soon take them on entirely different paths and move them apart for the first time in their young lives. Cicely became a nurse, moved to Corpus Christi, Texas, and spent her life as a single woman dedicated to her profession. Tarin had always been keenly interested in archaeology, and after earning her advanced degree in that field she moved to Cairo, Egypt, where she built a tremendous reputation working for the British museum there. Eventually, she met an English colleague, and though they did get married, the couple never had children and retired to a posh London flat where, both in their eighties, they still live today.

While her sisters were studying at Pitt, Olivia was never quite alone. But she had infinitely more freedom, solitude, and independence than she'd ever known previously. Finding herself the lone mistress of a large house, she had no intention of ever leaving. She began indulging herself in several long ignored interests and hobbies. Among those were cooking classical French cuisine and photography. Her late father's equipment lay unused in his basement studio for years until Olivia decided she wanted to take up that hobby. She did have some natural talent for taking very good photos, but it was nothing she could realistically make a career of, it was no more than a hobby for her. Yet, it pleasantly occupied her time, was interesting to her, and got her out of the house and taking pictures of her entire neighborhood as well as some very good nature shots. She particularly liked taking monthly photos of her favorite trees on the property. On the first day of each month, she would stand in the exact same spot as she photographed each tree. Soon enough, it was an impressive collection of an eclectic selection of images and topics that she had amassed, organized, and mounted in photo albums.

Oliver was listening intently to his aunt as it was, but upon hearing of these photo albums, his ears really perked up, and he immediately inquired as their whereabouts. Aunt Mary explained that they were here in the house up in that room referred to as the study. She felt his enthusiasm and knew he wanted to check that room out in detail, but she exhorted him to be patient. She would accompany him into the room because it was so special, filled with irreplaceable items and objects. For that fact alone, she asked him please not go in that room unsupervised. She promised to show him everything he was asking about that she could locate, just not right that minute. Somewhat disappointed but understanding his aunt's request, Oliver reluctantly but sincerely agreed to obey her wishes.

There was a special story she wanted to tell Oliver about Olivia, who as it turned out, was her mother! Olivia was living alone at the house as her student sisters were often away for days at a time staying with friends on or near their campus. Her interest in nature photography often took her into the woods across the valley, up the hill, and over the railroad tracks. There, the wood line was the start of some pretty dense woods that were home to deer, wild turkey, pheasant, rabbits, and just about any other wildlife indigenous to the area. It was also the outer fringe of an excellent area in which to do some hunting.

Well, one day, a fine cool, autumn day, Olivia was out in those woods actually hoping to photograph some of the great clumps of moss that grew in abundance on the southern side of so many trees there. She had bought a new lens for her dad's old camera, and it rendered even the smallest items viewable in amazing detail. As she was crouching down to get a better view of some uniquely orange lichen, she heard the snapping of twigs, and immediately recognized that sound as indicating that someone, quite likely a hunter, was very near and possibly coming her way.

She immediately called out and proclaimed her presence as a precaution against possibly being shot by some overzealous hunter. A loud *"Hello!"* was the response she received, and as she slowly rose up, she saw a young man whom she wasn't familiar with walking toward her with his rifle carried facing downward as a safety measure. He seemed to be roughly her age, and he was quite handsome and tall with wavy black hair. They simultaneously and perhaps instinctively smiled at each other, and in a moment, they were shaking hands and introducing themselves.

He was William Thompson from over the hill the other way in the township of Delaware. William was not only good looking and friendly, but he was educated and told her of being gainfully employed as a high school English teacher across the Allegheny River in the town of Oak Grove. Olivia, who had never gone to college, certainly didn't feel like the lesser being because she did, after all, bring quite a bit to table, as the saying goes. Nonetheless, she was truly impressed by this fellow, and everyone knows how important it is to make a good first impression since you only get one chance to do that with a new acquaintance.

Olivia invited William to accompany her home and promised to cook at least two of the several rabbits tied and thrown over his shoulder. Well, to make an otherwise long story short, this chance encounter was ultimately a classic example of love at first sight. Over a delicious supper at No. 1 Hughes Street, the two shared their individual stories, the conversation flowed smoothly, and there wasn't a hint of any awkward silence between them.

By the time they were finished eating and had cleaned up the dishes and kitchen, it was getting dark. Olivia offered to drive her new friend home. It was a long walk, and he could easily have made the hike, but he relented and accepted her offer. At his home, or his parent's home where he lived in the basement and paid a modest rent, the two agreed to see each other again, and soon. It was the fall of 1955, and Olivia was in love, for the very first time.

When she and William met again, they sat outside in the cool fall air with oversized sweaters on drinking hot tea and talking like you wouldn't believe. It was so easy for each of them to be with the other, and these two very new friends quickly realized that they wanted to be together a lot more . . . like for the rest of their lives.

So, on a frosty Saturday afternoon shortly after New Year's in January 1956, the two were married in small but rowdy ceremony at the old church up on the road to Pittsburgh. The event was rowdy because their friends were rowdy people, and loved a good party or any other reason to be loud and happy for that matter. This wedding was the perfect platform for such an occasion, for a raucous celebration. After a quick, three-day honeymoon trip to Niagara Falls, it was time for Christmas vacation to end and students and teachers reported back to school. Once the newlyweds were home in Rural Heights, when William returned home after school was dismissed for the day, they began a routine of driving over to William's parent's house where they loaded her car up with his possessions and transferred them to his new address. This only took a couple of days, and there was no need for him to bring furniture because that old house was filled with as much, even more furniture than two people would ever need.

Of course, Cicely and Tarin were always welcome there any time, but they were building their own lives now, and aside from the occasional school breaks, they generally stayed down on campus at Pitt. This left the happy couple to think about bringing someone else into their home to live with them. To that end in December of 1956, Olivia gave birth to a beautiful baby girl that the proud new parents almost naturally named Mary, or Aunt Mary, even Mom as her loving nephew Oliver now knew her. Oliver simply sat there in a happy cloud of contentment thinking on all this family history. Thoughts he never had before came flooding into his mind, and he was suddenly both proud and very happy to be part of such a great family, and family story. And he now rated history as his favorite class whenever anyone asked him.

It was the next Saturday and that meant getting up early, having a great big breakfast, and getting the yard work done with Uncle Dave before noon. There was no time to waste either because at one o'clock, they wanted to be at The Raven's Club just in time for lunch, and the Pitt game versus Notre Dame that was being televised. Oliver wanted to talk to Uncle Dave about the things he shared with Aunt Mary, but there was no time just then. It was also exactly one week until Oliver's thirteenth birthday. While they worked hard to get finished in the yard, Oliver was mentally ticking off a few of the most important questions he wanted to ask his uncle. He was quite curious about when Aunt Mary's parents left her that big house, the only house she'd lived in aside from going away to college. He also wanted to know when the two houses were built that were on what was originally part of their property. But these questions, despite begging for answers, could wait a little while longer.

Later that same Saturday afternoon, as Oliver and Uncle Dave pulled up into the driveway in the truck, Uncle Dave hit the garage door opener affixed to his sun visor at the perfect moment, and the two drove right into the garage even as the door was still going up. It was a driving feat that Oliver was never bored by, and truth be told, there was an impish side of that boy that sort of wished there would be a mishap, just one time. But in reality, he knew better and a bigger part of him was glad it never happened. Uncle Dave would have been pretty angry, and after all, he was Oliver's best friend in the world.

They were both in a pretty good mood. Pitt had defeated Notre Dame, and when Pitt won a football game, that was considered a good day in his uncle's book. They grabbed a couple of frosty root beers out of the man cave fridge, and after closing up the garage, they headed out— Uncle Dave toward the house and Oliver toward the old sycamore behind the garage. As they parted ways, Uncle Dave advised him that Aunt Mary would have supper ready within an hour, so the boy needed to be aware of the clock and allow himself ample time to get washed up before they ate. Oliver replied to this with a request to be called in time to do as his uncle asked.

Slipping that unopened root beer can into his hoody pouch, Oliver effortlessly ascended to that oh so familiar spot in his favorite tree. That ancient sycamore was as pleased as an arbor can be to have the youngster up in its branches once again, and the connection was immediate as Oliver relaxed and sipped on his can of root beer.

Aunt Mary turned out to be an only child in a marked departure from all the kids the two previous families had when they lived there. As a child, she had the complete run of the entire house and property, and while she was no delicate flower, the young Miss Mary was certainly no tomboy either. It was for that reason that her parents were so surprised the first time they saw her climbing up into that old sycamore behind the garage. They watched with some anxiety hoping that she wouldn't fall out of that tree and incur some broken bone or bones. When she didn't come down for quite a while, her father walked over to look up into those lofty branches and inquire as to his eight-year-old daughter's status way up there. When he was convinced she would be all right, he returned to his place beside his wife in their matching Adirondack lounge chairs a little way off under one of the old oak trees in the yard.

Oliver was definitely taken aback at hearing that his Aunt Mary used to climb up into this very same tree. He wondered if the tree *talked* to her as it did to him. That silent question would have made that old sycamore smile again if it were able to; this boy had that sort of effect on the venerable old tree. But the answer confused Oliver a bit. Yes, the tree communicated with his aunt during her childhood and just as it would be with Oliver. Once she reached her teen years, this experience would cease, and the memory of it all suddenly, yet softly, fades away. But that was a message for another time that was coming all too soon, for both of them, the boy and the tree.

Oliver was quietly content as the sycamore passed on tales of Aunt Mary's parents and how her dad had always been interested in foreign languages. For some reason, and a rather bizarre reason at the time, he had enrolled in classes at the University of Pittsburgh learning the Vietnamese language. No one knew it that time, but shortly, Vietnam, a country previously virtually unheard of unless one was familiar with its old colonial moniker of French Indo-China, was about to become a national obsession—a war against communism that dramatically divided America. In the meantime, William continued teaching by day and learning to speak Vietnamese three nights a week at Pitt. The year was 1961, and America had recently elected a new President, a handsome young man from Massachusetts, John Fitzgerald Kennedy or, as he soon came to be known, JFK.

Always a quick learner and an overall very intelligent man, William easily picked up this decidedly difficult language faster than any of his classmates, all six of them. His instructor, a World War II veteran named Dr. Banet', was impressed, and was also friends with the university's ROTC (Reserve Officer's Training Corps) commandant. It was Banet' who introduced those two, and from there, it was a simple matter of appealing to William's patriotic side. Political issues were getting dicey in Vietnam, and the communists were threatening to overrun the southern portion of that country, which wished to be a democracy. President Kennedy was being urged by his Cabinet to send over military advisors to bolster the South Vietnamese military efforts.

Discussions with his wife, Mary, had revealed to him her family's proud story of military service, and his own family could trace their contributions to America's military back to before America was even a sovereign nation, but a British colony. It wasn't a difficult decision, and both were actually excited at his prospects upon temporarily joining the military. After all, there wasn't actually a war going on that directly involved American troops, and all William would be doing is "advising" the side America was dedicated to supporting.

Based on his advanced level of education, which was a master's of education degree, and his easy comprehension of a difficult language only a precious few Americans even spoke, William was promised the rank of captain upon completing officer's basic training at Fort Benning, Georgia. When the current school year ended, William would be sent south for a twelve-week basic training course followed by another much more intensive Officer Training Course, which, upon completion, would earn him his captain's bars.

Just before Thanksgiving of 1962, when it was time for William's graduation and commissioning ceremony, his proud family drove down to Georgia to be in attendance. Olivia and young Mary were beaming with pride as their husband, daddy, and hero took his turn and walked across a stage to receive his commission as an officer and a gentleman in the United States Army.

Life went on as usual at No. 1 Hughes Street even with the man of the house almost nine thousand miles away. But things were never routine or normal for William during his service in Vietnam. As early as 1963, he began to have the bothersome suspicion that the United States had picked the wrong side to back in this dangerous contest, the intense struggle for a united Vietnam one way or the other, communist or democratic.

Captain Thompson saw things he would never be able to unsee in his mind's eye. He witnessed cruelty on an unparalleled scale that was absolutely shocking for the former high school English teacher whose only experience in seeing blood was from his hunting kills. Vietnam was different than anything he could have prepared for, and the extremes that the North Vietnamese or Viet Cong were willing to wreak upon their own countrymen to deter them from embracing democracy was stunning to him.

His fellow officers were no doubt as shocked as he was, but they were experienced soldiers. Some of the older advisors had fought in World War II, and Korea and told stories of horrific atrocities committed by both the Japanese and Germans in the "big war" as well the Chinese and North Koreans during that "little disagreement" as they referred to the conflict in Korea. Still, hearing such stories and witnessing those horrors in person were two different experiences, though very few of his cohorts revealed whatever *they* might have really been thinking, and William followed their example by being quiet and concentrating on training the South Vietnamese troops.

Then a tragic event occurred on November 22, 1963, that shocked the entire world and cast a pall over the national mood of the whole United States. John F. Kennedy, the youngest man ever to ascend to the office of the Presidency, was assassinated as he rode in a motorcade in an open vehicle through downtown Dallas, Texas. The young captain and his cohorts were as stunned as everyone else, but what no one fully realized at that time of national grieving was the irrefutable fact that neither America, nor the world would ever be the same again.

Captain Thompson slowly developed a rather keen dislike for his wards, which, upon reflection, fairly surprised him despite his earlier, more casual misgivings. He found the South Vietnamese soldiers to be more than a little detached from their mission, unmotivated, undisciplined, and lazy. Furthermore, they seemed to lack a certain moral courage or conviction. They were devoid of any deep seeded dedication to their cause, and as a result of these shortcomings they were repeatedly thrashed whenever they met their enemy in the jungles and rice paddies of Vietnam. By the time William's tour in Vietnam was finished in 1965, he was witness to tens of thousands of young Americans being drafted, quickly trained, and shipped off to the meat grinder that this miserable Asian nation had become.

He arrived home just in time for Christmas 1965, and his wife and daughter were fairly shocked at the man who returned to them. While William was always a very trim fellow, he had lost considerable weight over the past two years of service. His hair, at age thirty, was tinged with gray, his now thin faced easily showed his exhaustion and the stress he had experienced, and he often flinched at sudden, loud noises. However, the longer he was home, the easier things became for him, and he slowly but surely fell back into his old lifestyle . . . for the most part. In the fall of 1966, he returned to Oak Grove High School and resumed his previous position there as an English teacher.

While readjusting to civilian life gradually became easier overall for William, there were certain aspects of life in America at that time he could never quite accept. He never watched television during supper because the mealtime coincided with the evening news, and every day of the week, there were long casualty lists and live broadcasts replete with reports from front line combat areas that he just couldn't bear to watch. Furthermore, it bothered him greatly to know that all of his male students had to sign up for the draft when they turned eighteen. All over the country, on college campuses and in the cities, war protests were a regular occurrence and untold numbers of young

American men of military age illegally fled north to Canada to escape the draft.

William proudly noted that none of the boys he knew and taught avoided their duty in such a way, but it grieved him terribly to know something like 90 percent of those who were drafted were most likely going to Vietnam. Once again, his life was never going to be the same again, and little things he once took great pleasure in he now avoided almost completely. Watching his students playing football, basketball, and other sports once brought him a great deal of satisfaction, and although he didn't coach at all, it gave him great pleasure to watch his students compete athletically. It was after he received word that one of his former pupils had been killed in action in Vietnam that he subconsciously started planning to not attend those games as often as he had in the past.

Then, one day about three weeks afterward, as school ended for the day, and he was alone in his classroom, the school secretary delivered William a smudged, dirty envelope addressed to him in care of the school. Stamped on the envelope were the words "Damaged in action, Republic of Viet Nam." He studied it closely before carefully opening it, and he knew that the brown smudge was the blood of the letter's author. It was from that recently killed former student who, though an excellent football player, didn't quite have the grades to go on to college. Subsequently, the young man was drafted, became a United States Marine, and was killed in action thirty days short of his combat tour ending. The letter was short, but William could feel the desperation in that young man's writing, and it was particularly poignant when he ended his missive with this plea, "Please pray for me, tell the boys to study, and please don't ever forget me, sir."

William slowly stood up, walked over to his classroom door, closed and locked it, sat back down at his desk, and cried like he never had before. That same soldier's younger brother was playing football that night, and though he had been going to fewer games now, he decided he should go tonight. When he arrived at the stadium, William saw their father, a widower who looked so distraught, but stoically and with quiet dignity held his grief inside. William approached him, grasped his hand, and pulled the old man close for a hug that only those who have ever experienced such emotional trauma would ever understand. William, one of the original advisors sent to Vietnam, never attended another sporting event as long as he taught at that school. Oliver knew William as Grandpa Willie, and he really liked the old man. It saddened him to know how much pain a nice man like him carried around in his heart. The boy made a mental note to hug him a little longer the next time they met.

Part 16

Oliver Becomes a Young Man

Suddenly, Oliver heard Kathleen calling him to supper. Once again, it had gotten dark quickly and practically without notice, and it was time for Oliver to head back into the house. Lovingly patting that old tree's trunk as he walked away, Oliver thought on the revelation that Aunt Mary had once also climbed up into the very same branches that he so enjoyed now. Stepping into the warm light of the foyer, Oliver immediately sought out his aunt who was watching television with Kathleen and Uncle Dave in the living room, with dinner trays on their laps, eating supper. Kathleen had prepared a tray of food for Oliver, which he went and fetched from the kitchen. He then returned to the living room and sat by his beloved aunt and silently ate his supper. Afterward, he excused himself and went upstairs to take a shower and begin his nightly bedtime routine.

Oliver had never really thought much about it before, but he was suddenly aware that while he was in the shower, certain thoughts would often come into his head. A few times, answers to questions or the explanation about something that had been confusing him suddenly became quite clear. That night, it happened again, and the realization that what the tree had imparted to him about his aunt was essentially a secret, suddenly dawned on him, at the same time a vocabulary word that he was struggling with became clear *epiphany*. Now, he knew exactly what that strange word meant and had an excellent example of its meaning that he couldn't share with anyone else.

As is so often the case, one thought leads to another. Sometimes, it's just a tangent, an offshoot of the main idea or train of thought, and other times, it was simply the next step in a logical progression of thoughts. But at that moment, Oliver began to consider whether or not water, in this case his shower, could be the source or conduit for the answers to things that were confusing or misunderstood.

As the boy was coming out of the bathroom, the rest of the family was making their way upstairs to begin their nightly bedtime rituals. Oliver gave everyone a hug and a kiss good night and sort of whispered in his aunt's ear a request to sit with him in his room for a few minutes. So, as soon as Aunt Mary was ready for bed, she told Uncle Dave she was going to chat a few minutes with Oliver. Uncle Dave looked in the boy's room and asked if that conversation was private, or could he sit in as well. Oliver grinned and motioned for both his aunt and uncle, his Mom and Dad to enter his room.

As soon as the adults were seated, Oliver started right in by explaining that this wasn't something urgent or earth-shattering, but nonetheless, he was curious. When were the two houses built that were below their house? Furthermore, he was curious as to why they were built at all and wondered if it wasn't better before they were built when it was just one big house on one really big piece of property. Although Uncle Dave knew the answers to all these questions, he deferred to his wife who had spent most of her life living there at No. 1 Hughes Street.

Aunt Mary was once again smiling broadly as she listened to the thoughtful questions her favorite nephew, her son, was asking. She was smitten by his persistent quest for local history and information and thoroughly enjoyed their impromptu chats and discussions. These pleasant encounters and exchanges were just one of the many ties that bound them together so closely, and yet, there was a nagging question, a certain unknown aspect of his curiosity and line of questioning that prompted something in the very deepest recesses of her memory. But trying to figure out whatever *that* was would simply be a waste of time because she had been down that road many times trying to figure out that certain unknown. Oh well.

Uncle Dave and Oliver also had their own conversations and topics that they discussed. Oliver had previously posed questions to his uncle that he knew instinctively were topics generally reserved for men and boys, fathers and sons to discuss. They also discussed things like fishing, when Oliver could start going hunting with his uncle, and cars—because both of those fellows really liked cars. Oliver was dearly loved by his family, all of them, and he returned that precious love by being a great kid. He was kind, thoughtful, polite, and stayed out of trouble, and both Aunt Mary and Uncle Dave often commented on just how blessed they were that he had come into their lives.

"Oh my, yes," Aunt Mary said as she began to explain. "It was nicer when those two houses weren't here, but they were built for very good reasons."

The larger brick house was built because a very good friend of Grandma Olivia's. A Miss Samantha had made her and Grandpa Willie an offer to buy a corner piece of their property that they couldn't refuse. Grandpa was recovering from hip surgery and didn't get around as well as he used to; and besides, the money earned by the sale, which they didn't really need, it cut quite a bit off his yard workload. Oliver was familiar with Miss Samantha, but she had become a recluse in her old age and rarely ventured outside. As a result, unless you visited her at home, she was rarely seen. Furthermore, the old lady didn't really like visitors, so other than her family who did visit regularly, she kept almost entirely to herself.

The other house on the property, a smaller ranch-type home with no stairs or steps anywhere, was right by the road and on the bend coming up from the old River Road. It had actually been built by Grandma and Grandpa about fifteen years before. The reason for that house being built was because, as Aunt Mary had already told Oliver, Grandpa Willie had undergone hip surgery, and even though it had been a successful operation, he found it increasingly difficult to walk up and down stairs. Aunt Mary went on to explain that a smaller house with everything on one floor suited the aging couple perfectly, and after they moved in, the original big house was sold to Aunt Mary for the tidy sum of one dollar, plus whatever taxes and other expenses were attached to the bill of sale. Whatever that amounted to aside, it was one sweet deal she smilingly told him. Uncle Dave was smiling too and silently nodded his concurrence with that statement.

But Oliver knew that Grandma Olivia had passed away a few years ago, and her husband and companion of so many years was a resident of the Veterans' home up near Wolf Chapel. Now their little house was a rental property, and the rent received from their tenants went for taxes and into an account, which was exclusively for the venerable old man's personal use—except he rarely touched the money in it.

Oliver nodded at his aunt as she spoke to silently let her know he heard what she was saying and understood everything. But he was getting sleepy, and his eyelids were drooping, a sure sign that he was ready to fall asleep. And why not? It had been a busy day working in the yard all morning and the excitement of the game at the Raven's Club, and the cooler weather of fall that the area was experiencing made everyone sleep a little better at night. As they both stood up to leave, his aunt and uncle each bent over and kissed their beloved nephew and son good night, but he was already asleep.

Part 17

The Grand Old Sycamore
Is Officially Famous

After church the next day as the family arrived home, a slightly familiar car turned onto Hughes Street and steered over to the curb by the mailbox. Mrs. Wright, the driver, had her usual companions in tow, and they rolled down their windows to shout, "Yooohoooo!" up at Uncle Dave and get his attention. The four ladies definitely got his attention, and immediately, he started walking down the driveway in a trot to eliminate any possibility that they might actually *drive* up the driveway. Standing in place up in the yard and watching him hustle down to greet their visitors, Aunt Mary, Kathleen, and Oliver nudged each other and snickered a bit because *they knew* exactly what Uncle Dave was thinking.

When Uncle Dave had walked the ladies up to where his family awaited, Mrs. Wright introduced her companions or, as she coyly phrased it, her crew. Mrs. Ferlan, Mrs. Hurley, and Mrs. Bertolina were all there and apologized for intruding on a Sunday, but when they first met Uncle Dave and saw the sycamore tree, in their excitement, they neglected to ask for his phone number. So, they had to come in person, and they went on to say that they all felt it would be all right because after all, they came with great news. News that might be better served if revealed in the presence of that grand old tree.

As they gathered under the sycamore, Mrs. Bertolina, of whom the Uncle Dave suspected was second in command of this senior crew because she rode up front with Mrs. Wright, and, being the least formal member of her group insisted on being called Norie, began explaining that this tree was indeed a historic tree. It was one of the oldest in the country, in North America, in fact and record checks indicated it was one of the tallest as well. When Miss Norie finished her presentation of the tree's status, Oliver immediately chimed in and declared to everyone that this tree had witnessed events both great and small since the eighteenth century. All nodded and murmured their agreement with the boy's claim. Just to drive his point home and give everyone a little something to think about, he finished by adding, "Can you imagine the stories this tree would tell if only it could talk?"

Already imagining what that tree might say, if it could, everyone was just nodding and looking at the sycamore.

Politely declining Aunt Mary's invitation to stay for some lunch, the four ladies were walked to their car by Uncle Dave. Mrs. Wright concluded the visit, as she started her car, by telling him that before Halloween, she and her crew would be back with officials from the Arbor Society, and assured him that this time, they had his phone number and would certainly call first. The purpose of that visit would be to present the tree, and of course, Uncle Dave with what she described as a handsome bronze plaque mounted on a carved marble block that would be permanently placed close to the tree. That plaque would remind or inform everyone who would ever see it the exact significance of that magnificent old tree. Miss Norie spoke up one last time to advise Uncle Dave to consider getting some insurance coverage just in case anything unseemly should ever be visited upon this living treasure. He smiled and waved as the quartet of elderly tree lovers pulled onto the road and drove away.

Walking back up the driveway, Uncle Dave was waited for by Oliver who, when his uncle was close enough and the boy wouldn't have to shout, said, "You should have seen yourself getting down to their car before they started to drive up here."

Uncle Dave smiled at his nephew, but really, it was no joking matter to this man so devoted to keeping his yard as perfect as possible. He put his arm around his favorite nephew, his son, and they walked together into the house.

After lunch, Oliver changed into his jeans and a T-shirt, slipped into his sneakers, and ambled out the door and across the yard to the tree. It had never been *just a tree* to him or anyone else in the family, but suddenly, it was a celebrity, a tree of noteworthy prominence and so important that it might even be getting insured! Oliver was almost to the tree when his friend, Salvatore, or Sal as he was universally known, was riding his bike up the driveway yelling to Oliver that he should get his bike. As Sal pulled up to the top of the driveway with his ever-present backpack with a football inside, he told Oliver that all their friends were meeting at the schoolyard to play football in a few minutes.

Oliver assured Sal he would be there forthwith, but that he had to tell his folks where he was off to. Sal held up his thumb in the okay signal and sped off down the driveway around the bend and out of sight. After telling Aunt Mary and Uncle Dave where he was going, Oliver trotted out toward the garage and the sycamore, stopping ever so briefly to place his hand on that tree's rough bark, and silently apologized for running off like this. He then went into the garage, mounted his bike, and raced off to meet up with his friends. The boy's thirteenth birthday was just six days away.

Later that afternoon, as Aunt Mary was up in the study looking through some of the old photo albums she had promised to show Oliver, she once again happened to glance out the window. Immediately, her gaze fell upon the sycamore, that noble tree that had stood out there in the yard even before it was a yard. She thought for a moment on something Oliver had once said about their yard once being a grove of sorts, or maybe just a group of trees, but consisting of many more trees than were out there now. She *knew* that to be true, although she couldn't quite rationalize how or why she did. Over the years, she had spent many pleasant hours poring over nearly all the papers, books, photos, and whatever else was in that room, and the answer, to the best of her knowledge, did not lie within those four walls. She looked away and resumed leafing through those dusty old photo albums.

By the time Oliver got home from playing with his friends, it was suppertime, and he dutifully washed up and ate with his family. He was excited that his aunt told him she had located the old photo albums he wanted to see and had selected several she thought he might like to peruse with her after the table was cleared and the dishes done. Uncle Dave voiced his wish to look those albums over as well, but Kathleen thought it was all boring and went up to her room to watch television by herself.

So there they were, just the three of them huddled around a corner of their big, old dining room table sitting before a stack of long neglected albums. Somewhat disappointed by the fact that not one of the photos they looked at that night were in color, Oliver was nonetheless visibly moved by the variety and overall excellent quality of the pictures contained therein. Grandma Olivia had possessed some serious photographic skills after all, and most of those photos were quite clear and focused, if not turning more than a little yellow. Shots of the house from several angles showed the whole yard as it was before the two relatively recent houses were built on the property. The subject content included images of family and friends, local events, special occasions, and almost every building and house in the entire community right up until Grandma Olivia had finally weaned herself off of her photographic passion and concentrated on her family.

There was an entire album dedicated to just the trees in their yard, and there were several shots of each taken at various times of the year and over a period of years. In every one of those images, the sycamore stood out. As everyone who ever saw it would attest, one never realized just how big and majestic that tree was until you viewed it from a distance. Of course, standing beside it made everyone seem diminutive but going up on the hill, the Heights, and looking down toward the property at No. 1 Hughes Street, the aged sycamore absolutely dominated the entire property, towering over everything.

There was one photo in particular that Oliver was smitten with. It must have been taken from across the valley and up the hill behind the railroad tracks. In that photo, the house could not be clearly seen, for all the trees in front of it from that perspective, but the unmistakable crown of the sycamore stretched magnificently up to the sky above everything else. Aunt Mary remarked how much she liked that specific photo as well. Spending quality time with his aunt and uncle checking out some family history was the perfect way to end the weekend, but now, it was time for bed. Tomorrow was another start to another school week.

Part 18

All Good Things Must End

Being his birthday week necessarily meant that the days fairly dragged by for Oliver, and it seemed like Friday and the end of this school week would never arrive. But it did, finally, and as Oliver got off the school bus and started trudging up the hill to his house, just as it was pulling away, the entire busload of kids had pulled down their windows on one side and shouted in unison, "Happy birthday, butthead!" Oliver turned back to look at them and grinning hugely, he waved them off.

His birthday was tomorrow, but somehow, he wasn't really thinking about it too much right then. Something had been gnawing at his subconscious, not in a bad way, but definitely in a persistent manner. He couldn't stop trying to figure out what it was, and the whole thing was a huge distraction. He headed directly to the sycamore, and dropping his backpack at its base, he quickly climbed up into his spot. Once there, he felt an almost physical sensation overcome him, and he welcomed it because it was the reason; this is what had been bugging him. He didn't really know quite why, but nonetheless, Oliver instantly realized that he needed to be with his tree at this very moment. The spectacular old sycamore was equally pleased, and without delay, began silently communicating with the boy.

Somehow, that old tree just knew of the conversations Oliver had with his Aunt Mary and that they had viewed those old photo albums. The sycamore was even more pleased and somewhat relieved

135

because, although much of what was to be imparted to Oliver by the tree remained unfinished, the task had been completed nonetheless and done very well too. Oliver was thinking on all the events over all of the years of its existence that this wonderful tree had *shown* him. There was a timeline of events being flashed through the boy's brain, courtesy of the sycamore, and he actually saw everything of significance that this historic natural edifice had witnessed over the two hundred or so years of its existence.

No sooner was this mental history lesson completed when Oliver heard Uncle Dave calling up to him, "Is this your backpack, or does our old tree here go to school too?"

Good old Uncle Dave, he made Oliver smile and the tree relaxed as well, "No, it's me, Dad, just hanging out up here for a few. I'm coming down, hang on please."

With that, the boy patted his sturdy old friend and quickly descended out of those lofty branches that still had an impressive number of leaves to drop. Uncle Dave handed Oliver his backpack, and they walked toward the house together.

After supper and just for a few minutes before it got dark, Oliver slipped back up into that tree. There was still a wee bit of something bugging him, but he couldn't quite put his finger on what it might be. In those all too brief few minutes, the sycamore once again let Oliver *see* a few things from its past. As he lay back and closed his eyes, scene after scene passed through his mind, but there were a few flashes that made him stop, open his eyes, and sit up. It was Aunt Mary as a young girl, maybe eight years old or so. There were more visions of her as she was growing up! She was climbing up into this very tree! She was sitting, no, reclining just as he always did, smiling, and nodding! This old sycamore had communicated with his aunt when she was about his age! This ever-present witness tree had shown her almost everything that it had shown Oliver. Such a revelation begged the question about why she had never told him about this, these unwittingly shared experiences. But in fact, the boy already *knew* why, he had merely forgotten. That's how the trees worked.

Then, every boy and girl who had ever climbed into the sycamore's branches was shown to him, even if it were just one time.

Those flashing images slowed somewhat whenever they were of a child the tree had communicated with, and there were actually several, but that hardly made Oliver feel any less special. He felt very secure in his place in this tree's life. He only wished he could talk to and share experiences with all those kids from years gone by.

Suddenly, it was all over, and there were no more mental images, no more unspoken messages. Oliver sat up and sensed something, no, he sensed nothing. Whatever was happening just a moment ago was over, gone, and he struggled a bit to get those thoughts or whatever they were back. Try as he might to bring back or reignite his experience it was all for naught, and all he did was create confusion and bewilderment within himself.

It was dark, and Oliver no longer felt like being up in that tree. He sat alone up in his spot thinking why he liked being there so much. Again, there was no real answer to that question, his mind simply told him that he just did. Feeling just a bit foolish, Oliver gathered himself and made his way down out of that tree. He was feeling a bit foolish because as of midnight tonight, he would be thirteen years old; certainly he was not just a little kid anymore.

He'd thought on this earlier today at school as he combed his hair in the locker room mirror after gym class. Yes, he was a year older, but he didn't feel any older, nor did he see any particular physical changes, he still looked like he was twelve years old. He stood at the base of the old sycamore, one hand open and touching the tree, totally distracted by his thoughts and oblivious to anything else at that moment.

Suddenly, there was a firm but gentle hand on his shoulder, and a slightly startled Oliver spun around to see his Aunt Mary standing before him smiling. "I've been calling you for ten minutes. Your friend, Salvatore, called and wants you to call him back."

Oliver sighed, and simply replied, "All right, thank you."

With that, Oliver and his aunt started to walk across the yard toward the house. As they were about to step out of the darker shadow cast by that big old tree, a deep voice, strong but certainly not menacing was suddenly heard to say, "Hello again, Mary, and thank you, Oliver."

The pair stopped and looked at each other. "Did you hear something?"

Aunt Mary asked her nephew. Oliver was grinning in the darkness, but completely uncertain as to exactly why, so he technically wasn't lying when he responded, "No, I didn't hear anything." Suddenly and silently, a couple of sycamore tree balls fell and gently hit them as they started to walk away again.

"No, I guess I didn't either. It must've been the wind," said his aunt.

As they walked, Oliver put his arm around his aunt and hugged her close and tight. "I love you, Mom," he said sincerely.

Suddenly noticing how tall her nephew/son had become, his aunt replied, "I love you too, Oliver. Let me be the first to wish you a happy thirteenth birthday. You are certainly becoming quite the fine young man."

"33"

About the Author

R D Slover is a man with a past. He has been at various times in his life a US Army tank commander in Germany, a USPS letter carrier, a trained and certified chef, University of Pittsburgh graduate with a degree in history, a teacher, extra in the movie *Gettysburg*, and the proud father of four great kids.

His love of and knowledge of history and the intriguing concept of "witness trees," that is living trees that were present during and witness to significant historic events, were the seed from which this book was born.

Equally inspiring were the author's young grandson, Oliver, upon whom the main character is based. Your humble scribe continues to indulge his own fascination with the past by being an avid reader, travelling extensively throughout the United States, Canada, and Europe.

Although Mr. Slover was born in Texas and spent most of his life calling Pittsburgh, Pennsylvania, home, he now resides in a quiet little farming community on the southern prairie of western Canada with his wife Gwen, two eccentric cats and a rotund, very spoiled Pug.

CPSIA information can be obtained
at www.ICGtesting.com
Printed in the USA
BVHW090940200519
548791BV00018B/1724/P